The
Mystery Book
Mystery

The
Mystery Book
Mystery

Wylly Folk St. John

The Viking Press   New York

1 2 3 4 5 80 79 78 77 76

Library of Congress Cataloging in Publication Data
St. John, Wylly Folk.   The mystery book mystery.
Summary: Seventeen-year-old Libby Clark signs up
for a writers' conference on mysteries and becomes
entangled in a real-life murder mystery.
[1. Mystery and detective stories. 2. Authors—Fiction]
I. Title. PZ7.S1434Mw   [Fic]   75–37596

ISBN 0–670–50260–x

Contents

4/25/76

This book, with love, is for my husband, Tom,
who helps me so much in so many ways

The
Mystery Book
Mystery

1

*Tuesday Night
and Back to Monday*

It's just about midnight.

I finished typing out on my Hermes: "The Mystery Book Mystery. By Libby Clark." I rolled the paper out and put in another sheet, typed "Page One" and then "Chapter One." I started listing the characters.

Victim: Carlton Gillespie, locally famous columnist and successful slick-magazine writer. First novel about to come out in hardcover. At Piedmont Foothills Writers' Conference as star speaker for the Awards Dinner. Won Forrester Prize as newspaper reporter eleven years ago for local exposé of communist activities in Alabama, in connection with Soviet buildup in Cuba.

Found strangled and with the back of his head bashed in—

Then I stopped and took a deep, horrified breath. Could I do it? I had seen him lying there. He was the first dead man I ever saw—television doesn't count, of course— except Uncle Al, who lay neatly in his coffin, with every-body saying, "Doesn't he look natural?" Mr. Gillespie's body wasn't neat, and he didn't look natural. (Neither did Uncle Al, for that matter.) Can I write a mystery story about a real murder, just as if it were fiction?

Well, that's what I came here for—to learn how to write mysteries. That's what writers' conferences are for. I guess. They have a staff of experts to advise on any kind of writing you want to learn. Mr. Hamlyn Brent is the conference's expert on mysteries.

The police detective told us politely just to go on with our little convention, only don't anybody leave the cam-pus. Everybody is to be available for questioning at any time. The detective's name is Lieutenant "Dopey" Ayres, according to our campus security guard, Mr. Bridgewater, a good friend of mine. The reason for the lieutenant's nickname isn't what you'd think—it's because he once rounded up a dope ring. The name is meant as a sort of compliment, Mr. Bridgewater says, deadpan.

Mr. Hamlyn Brent had told us, at the first mystery workshop, before the murder happened, that we were all to turn in an idea for a mystery novel by the third day of the conference. So I asked him, as soon as I could catch him alone after Mr. Gillespie's body was taken away, if he thought it might be a good plan to use *this* mystery for my book? Because I knew just a few little things that maybe even the police didn't know.

He said with a private kind of smile that he'd thought of using it for a book himself, but for me to go ahead. He would let me have all rights to the idea. "By the way, what is it you know that the police don't?" he asked.

"I'd better keep that a secret, to see if you guess it in my book," I told him with my own private kind of smile. "I can't tell if it's any good, can I, as to the 'element of suspense,' unless it keeps you—the reader—guessing?"

He just shrugged and looked faintly amused. I don't think Mr. Hamlyn Brent believes I can write a book, because I'm only seventeen—even though my S. A. T. score was so high I got into college last year without having to take senior year in high school. I'm nearly eighteen now and I've just got to show him I can do a great mystery.

I thought of using "The Bible Verse Mystery" for my title, because of the verse cut out of somebody's Bible that Mr. Gillespie had pinned to his chest. The body, I mean, had pinned to *its* chest. It was a weird obscure verse: "No man shall take the nether or the upper millstone to pledge, for he taketh a man's life to pledge." It makes chills go up my spine. ". . . he taketh a man's life . . ." I also thought of calling my book "The Case of the Nether Millstone," because Mr. Gillespie's body was lying stone cold dead on the millstone in the Founders' Garden when I went out there early this morning.

But somehow I like "The Mystery Book Mystery" best. That first day, before the real murder part started, Mr. Brent said at our opening workshop session that it's always good to use the word "mystery" in the title. I figure if one "mystery" is good, two ought to be even better. And it's appropriate, even if it does sound like double talk until you know what I mean.

That first day, too, Mr. Brent gave us some rules for

writing mysteries. The first rule is to play fair with the reader. Let him in on absolutely everything that happens. So I think the best way will be for me to write down every night every single thing that happens that day. Then the reader will know as much as the author about it. And right at this point in time, as you-know-who used to say on TV, the reader knows as much as anybody. Because nobody knows who killed Mr. Carlton Gillespie—except the one who did it, of course. The police haven't the remotest idea.

I realize that the author is supposed to know who the murderer is before she starts writing the book, but how could I? I certainly didn't do it. At this point the one I'd pick out of the whole bunch, just from the way he looks and all, is Mr. Jim Phillips, alias Phillip James. But of course the most likely one is hardly ever the guilty one. Jim Phillips wears a turning-gray beard, and he's thin and dark and tall and ugly. He's a fascinating Dr.-Jekyll-and-Mr.-Hyde kind of writer; he writes for religious magazines and inspirational book publishers as "Phillip James," and as "Jim Phillips" he writes those lurid sexy paperbacks with covers that always show a girl's clothes being torn off —whether it happens in the book or not.

There are two of Jim Phillips's recent ones on display in the lobby downstairs, along with the "works" of all the other authors present at the conference. They're all spread out on a huge table—Phillips's *Now I Lay Me Down* and *The Horizontal Streaker* between Van Saylor's *The Black Labor Problem* and *Prize Forrester Prize Stories,* the new collection including Mr. Carlton Gillespie's long-ago Forrester Prize series from the *Birmingham Star-Banner.* I notice more of the conference people pick up *The Horizontal Streaker* than ever pick up *The Black Labor Problem* or the prize collection. Or even the copies of *Cosmopolitan* and *Redbook* that have Mr. Gillespie's latest published stories in them. Or even Elaine Westover's heavy love poetry that she had a vanity publisher fix up in a scarlet-and-gold binding.

Elaine Westover is here to talk to the poetry group studying under Fleetwood Barr. But I don't see how she could have strangled Mr. Gillespie and bashed his head in, even though he was rather small for a man. He was slim and dark and dapper, wore a thin mustache, and waxed it and his eyebrows to turn upward. But he must surely have been stronger than Miss Westover—unless she's taken judo or something. (Check on that possibility.) Anyway, why would she want to kill him? Mr. Brent says every suspect has to have a motive. (Check on motives.)

If the most *un*likely person is to be the murderer—as so frequently happens in mystery stories I've read—I would have to pick Mr. Hamlyn Brent himself. He is an aloof kind of man from New York, where I think he makes the literary scene practically by himself. He looks a lot like Mephistopheles, with a sharp, sardonic face, olive skin that just misses looking tanned, dark hair that grows back leaving two points on his forehead, and *Esquire* kind of clothes. He stays apart from the rest of the staff and the "writers" at the conference, observing them like a bird watcher or something, making mental notes and not-smoking unlit cigarettes poised elegantly in a long black holder. He never mingles and talks to anybody. He even eats by himself. He couldn't be interested in anything but the fee he gets for spending this week holding the mystery workshop. He couldn't be interested enough in any individual here to commit a murder. Could he? (Yet he *did* try to find out what I knew that the police didn't.)

Anyway, he does agree that I ought to put down every clue as it comes along (and that'll be a help to him if he really needs to know all I know!), so I guess I'd better go back and start at the beginning, which was yesterday morning—Monday, the day the conference started.

I got there early, carrying my Hermes in one hand and my suitcase in the other. They don't have bellhops at the Alabama Center for Continuing Education.

The center is a sort of barnlike hotel on the college campus where various educational conferences are held, and big meetings of all sorts that have any educational tie-in. This week an Egg-Laying Advisory for the College of Agriculture is being held too, and the members wearing poultry badges sometimes get mixed up and check in at the poetry room with Mr. Barr and Miss Westover.

I registered and went up to my room, 325, on the third floor. As I approached, key in hand, I caught just a glimpse of the back of a tall man I didn't recognize, going into 327. Well, at least I wasn't going to have two people yakking next door, I congratulated myself. Room 325 isn't the kind you'd want to spend much time in, what with the cigarette burns on the furniture and carpets, and the Gideon Bible on the dresser, so I wandered down to the lobby as soon as I had fixed my face.

The first thing that struck my eye was the poster calling attention to the "works" of the writers who were on the program for the various workshops and panel discussions. That large table held a great many books and magazines besides *Now I Lay Me Down* and *The Horizontal Streaker* —but I was drawn in fascination straight to those two. I admit it. I stood there and read a few pages—and kept on reading.

"Are you interested in writing paperback books?" a voice said politely, and I looked up to see a man mentally taking my temperature from the opposite side of the table. He didn't look very exciting—middle-aged, average-faced, ordinary, wearing a greenish sports coat that was a subdued plaid, I guess, but not very.

"No. No, sir," I said, putting the book down hastily. "I was just looking." He too had on a conference badge, and I squinted to read it.

"I'm Van Saylor," he said. "I'm holding the nonfiction workshop. I was hoping you were interested in nonfiction."

"No. I want to write mysteries," I told him, not even apologetically. My eye fell on the hefty volume next to the couple of sexy ones—the author's name. "You wrote this?" I said doubtfully. *"The Black Labor Problem"?*

"Yes," he acknowledged modestly. "You wouldn't have read it, of course? It's a radical study of union labor from the black workingman's point of view."

That was so much double talk to me. I had thought of labor, when I thought of it at all, as what happened to women who didn't take the Pill and then had scruples about abortion. How to get away from a man who wrote on such a subject? Come to think about it, he did look sort of like a radical, though he didn't have a beard or mustache. His face looked naked, without any hair at all on it when almost everybody else around had some, even if it was only a Confucius-tuft like Mr. Fletcher Barr's. But where did he get the black workingman's point of view?

"No. I like stories—I don't read much nonfiction," I said candidly, hoping that would make him realize that he wouldn't be interested in me; I'm no Lolita. I smiled at him politely, a goodbye sort of smile, and edged away from the table. But he came along with me as I drifted out into the main lobby.

"Do you know all these people?" he asked, nodding toward the small groups sitting and standing around, waiting for lunch, nearly everyone wearing the conference badge proudly. There were a few who looked as though they might be real writers—the kind that at least occasionally manage to have something published and get paid for it. But on the whole they looked like a pretty hopeless lot: college magazine editors wearing big metal-rimmed glasses, and eager young would-be poets (I knew a few of the college ones), middle-aged women who had wanted to write all their lives and were just now getting around to it after the children got married and before the grandchildren came, older men who had recently retired and had to find something respectable to do with their spare time or their wives would find it for them, and a few eccentric-looking characters, male and female, with no special category except that they were usually talking at great length about whatever rocks happened to be rattling around in their skulls. There were also a few keen kids like me, journalism students at the college who came to the conference for some neat course such as the mystery writing or the TV writing course. That last is a very popular one. The word has gotten around in college literary circles that TV is panting to pay huge sums of money to prolific young writing geniuses. I bet.

"No," I answered Mr. Saylor. "I don't know any of them. I just got here." I figured I might as well let him brief me on them, since he seemed to be going to stick around with me anyhow. "Let's sit down here and you tell me about them."

"I don't know them either," he said, sitting beside me on a vacant sofa nevertheless. "Except the staff people. We had a little preliminary get-together last night and I met most of them."

"Then tell me about those. Which is Hamlyn Brent? He has the mystery workshop I'm here for."

He nodded toward Mr. Brent, and I had my first sight of him sitting moodily apart on an uncomfortable-looking modernistic hassock, observing the passing scene as though he didn't think much of it. Now and then he scowlingly glanced at his long cigarette-holder that had that unlit cigarette in it. He was clearly exercising his will power on the cigarette, knowing cigarettes were bad for his lungs, but realizing that temptation might overcome him any minute—and when it did he didn't want to waste any time fiddling around finding one and fitting it into the holder.

"He's written dozens of mystery novels," Mr. Saylor said. "But they say he's about written himself out—he hasn't published one in some time. Or why would he waste time coming to a thing like this? The fee's not enough to attract any successful writer."

9

I started to ask, "Why did you come, then?" but stopped myself in time.

He answered anyway. "Oh, I'm not a successful writer. I never was. A two-hundred-dollars-and-board fee is all right for me to pick up for a dull week in summer when I'm not doing anything else. It's better than research, for God's sake. But the popular ones ought to be able to do better than that. Carlton Gillespie, for instance." He nodded toward a group centered on the man with the noticeable eyebrows and pointed beard and waxed mustache who turned out to be—who else?—the famous Alabama writer. "Of course it's easy to see why he came. Pure ego. He'd go anywhere and make a speech to anybody. Because he's got a hardcover book coming out at last, and he laps up publicity."

"I've seen his one-shot novels in magazines." I gestured toward the "works." "And the new collection with his prize series in it, of course. But I didn't know he'd done a real novel."

"He's correcting the galleys this week," Mr. Saylor said cynically. "Very ostentatiously. This morning he was doing it at breakfast. He's started writing mysteries, too. Had one in last month's—*Ellery Queen,* was it? Or *Cosmopolitan?* And Maude Ruskin was telling me he's working on a hardcover mystery now. Very versatile guy, isn't he?" he commented in a sardonic tone I didn't understand. Carlton Gillespie *was* versatile, no doubt about it. "Do you read his column?" he ended.

"Doesn't everybody?" In Alabama one's day hasn't started until one has read "Gil's Day" in the *Birmingham Star-Banner.* "And who's the good-looking faded-a-bit blonde?"

10

"That's Mrs. Gillespie. June. Surely you've read *ad nauseum* in the column about 'June-Bug'?" He showed a slight edge of disdain.

"Oh. That's Mel's mother?"

Now I *was* interested. I knew Mel Alston, of course. And I liked him. He would be football captain next fall. He had been in some of my classes last semester, making up stuff he'd flunked, and I had had a few exploratory dates with him. He's Mrs. Gillespie's son by her first husband, long out of the picture. There's a Gillespie daughter, too, I remembered, Mel's half-sister Carla. But she goes to Radcliffe.

"Watch this," Mr. Saylor said out of the corner of his mouth. "It should be interesting."

"Why interesting?"

"She's Elaine Westover. Mr. Gillespie likes her—more than Mrs. Gillespie does." The significant look he gave me could well pass for a leer until he practiced up on a better one.

Approaching the Gillespie group was a woman who reminded me of what they said about Snow White in the fairy story: white as snow, black as night, red as blood. Her skin was very pale, her eyes and hair very black, and her lips very red. She was tall and slim and looked like a willow tree walking. She was considerably older than Snow White, though—at least thirty. Maybe more.

Miss Westover just nodded at the Gillespies and passed them by serenely, going to sit graciously with a gabble of ladies who welcomed her with clucking admiration. Seeing that at this point the name Elaine Westover meant absolutely nothing to me, Mr. Saylor explained, "She writes passionate poetry. She's one of Fleetwood Barr's guest speakers, because she's an Alabama poet. The poetry is published by a vanity publisher, of course." He sneered.

"Her latest book—didn't you notice it on display with the others over yonder?—is called *Poems of Love and Rage.*" He seemed to take a dim view of rage and love, though I suspected he might have been susceptible to a personal touch of Miss Westover if he'd had the chance, which wasn't likely. "She had the Apollo Press do it up in a red-hot binding—you almost expect to see smoke curling up from it—and she dedicated it to C. G."

"How indiscreet of her," I murmured, looking around some more and wondering how Mr. Saylor had managed to gather so much information about the others in one evening. "Are you an Alabama man, Mr. Saylor?"

"I used to live in Birmingham—some years ago. But I'm based in New York now."

"Then how do you know all about—"

"I listen to gossip," he admitted frankly, almost proudly.

"Well—" I accepted his bragging with only one lifted eyebrow, and went on. "I know Professor Hawes, of course, but who are the two women with him?"

Professor Leslie Hawes had been new here at the college last semester. He had come over from Auburn to be head of the history department. He taught me English history, and I passed. On the side, he writes pretty good historical novels. They'd sell better if they had more sex in them than history, but the Professor just doesn't seem much interested in sex—or in writing about it. Which is odd, because he's a very sexy-looking guy. He's big and broad-shouldered and black-haired, with a sensitive face and soft gray eyes. He's married and has three small children, or I'd be even more interested in him than I am.

"The smart gray-haired woman is Serena Wilcox," Mr. Saylor explained, and I realized how flatteringly I was making him feel important, letting him display his familiarity with the staff. "She's holding the workshop in slick-magazine fiction. She writes women's stuff. Very popular. The other one, the stout little competent-looking one, is Maude Ruskin, who's giving the lecture on agents. She's a very successful New York agent, they say—though again, I can't see why she'd be here if she had anything better to do."

"There's Dr. Mark Petersen, though," I pointed out, suddenly wanting to deflate Van Saylor. "He's an Alabama man, and he's giving the novel workshop—and I know he's got better things to do. Maybe they like to help writers." I love Dr. Petersen, who is head of the English department and has taught a surprising number of his students here how to write successful novels. He's worked on me, too, from time to time. But he says I don't burn with enough of the holy ardor to be a real genius.

"Oh, I guess they get enough out of it to make it worth their time, the ones who are already at the college anyway," Van Saylor said grudgingly. "Like Silvanus Crossett and Larry Mims." They're both faculty members; Dean Crossett is director of this conference, and Mr. Mims is holding the drama workshop. TV plays, though, are being taught by a well-known New York playwright named Cobb Wilmer. I had already had him pointed out to me by Frank at the desk as I came in, but Mr. Wilmer was red-haired and not very attractive and I didn't want

13

to write TV plays anyhow. He was talking to Dean Crossett. The Dean's a stout gentleman who looks like Falstaff in a business suit with a largish black bow tie—and I thought Mr. Wilmer was complaining about something. Probably the lack of service; this center isn't exactly the Paradise-Hilton. There isn't any bar—only a coffee shop with a soda fountain. That lack would probably just about crucify a New York TV playwright, I figured.

Larry Mims stood with them, looking sallow and bored, as usual, and as if he were trying—not quite successfully —to keep his consciousness tuned to Tennessee Williams.

"There comes the man who wrote those paperbacks you were so interested in," Mr. Saylor said. "He looks vaguely like somebody I've met somewhere. He wasn't at the coffee klatch last night, or I'd have asked him if we've met." He ruminated a moment—and I do mean ruminated; he chewed the possibility over in his mind. "Jim Phillips or Phillip James," he went on, with that same touch of envious scorn I had noticed before in him, "depending on whether he's being sexy or religious. I guess they're both pen names, actually. Mine is, too," he added, but if he was trying to interest me in his real self—well, I couldn't have cared less.

"Who's the guy with him?" I asked. He was a strange-looking boy with a thin, intense face, wild yellow hair all over it as well as on his head, reddish-brown eyes like a fox's, and wearing a dingy pair of jeans and a rumpled T-shirt.

"I don't know," Van Saylor admitted. "He must be a Writer. He wasn't at the staff thing last night."

"I think I'll go and see," I said. I rose swiftly from the sofa and escaped before he could offer to go with me.

14

"See you at the picnic tonight, then," he called after me.

Not if I see you first, I said silently as I followed the bearded boy into the coffee shop. He wasn't actually with Jim Phillips; Mr. Phillips went on past the coffee-shop door, with a brusque nod to the boy, who dropped down wearily at the first vacant table. There were lots of people in the place, which gave me a chance to stop at his table and ask him, "Do you mind if I sit here?"

He just nodded; he didn't stand up or welcome me at all. But I sat down anyway, because I was curious, and because I wanted some coffee.

He wasn't wearing a badge like the lady Quillwriters of Anniston, Alabama, and all the other conference people, but he looked more like a writer than an egg-laying devotee. "I'm Libby Clark," I said, feeling ridiculously as though I were putting all my cards on the table and hadn't another qualification up my sleeve.

He didn't even volunteer his name until I said, "You're —" and then he grunted, "I'm Dory Pevlin." Somehow it sounded as though he thought everybody ought to know who Dory Pevlin was. But there was no reason at all why anybody should.

The girl brought the coffee—his and mine—and we both drank it black. That should have given us something in common, but no. I don't usually have any trouble getting a man to start a conversation with me, but there must have been something wrong with me yesterday. Dory Pevlin just sat there drinking coffee as if it were arsenic, and paying absolutely no attention to me. He wasn't the least bit attractive, and I don't know why I should have minded, but it was a sort of challenge, I guess. I said ingenuously, "What do *you* write?"

He let his eyes insert their glance into mine as if he were deliberately placing a piece of thin steel where he wanted to slide it in.

"I don't write," he said after a while, morosely. "I live. Sometimes I bleed—onto paper. Then it's a story. Sometimes I bleed—onto canvas. Then it's a painting."

I kept myself from laughing. But I couldn't think of a really apt comment. So I asked aimlessly, "Are you married?"

"Married!" He was as vehement denying it as though I had accused him of being intolerant of the Gay Liberation movement. "My analyst says I'll be free of the mother image in another six months. The father image may take a little longer. Then when I get loose from my transference to the analyst himself I'll be free. What would I want to get married for?"

I didn't feel like going into all that right then. Let his analyst tell him. "Well, it's an experience," I said without much originality. "Writers ought to know every experience there is."

"Yes. You know that?" He looked at me with a gleam of interest at last. "Yes. I think they should. Even murder, you know. I'll probably kill somebody someday. Just to feel how it is to murder. A man or—a woman—" He looked speculatively at me. I shivered.

"Everybody is capable of murder," Dory Pevlin went on. "Did you know that? If the provocation is enough, *any*-body could kill. *You* could."

"Oh, I just want to write about it," I said positively. "Not do it. I can satisfy my murderous impulses by writing about them. Do you write murder stories?"

"Is Genesis a murder story?" He brooded for a moment. "Yes. I write stories with murder in them. And many other forbidden things."

"Are they—published?" I asked as delicately as I could. "What magazines? I'd like to read them."

"Most magazines wouldn't touch them," he said contemptuously. "But I had a personal letter from the editor of *New Directions* once. Rejecting my sketch."

"I can't help wondering what you're doing here," I said. "I don't think they're having any workshop that fits your stuff exactly. Dr. Petersen wouldn't even try to teach you to bleed more salably."

"I ask myself the same thing," he said somberly, missing my joke. "What am I doing here? I exist. That's all. My mother provided the money. I can exist here as well as anywhere else. But these stupid people—no. It was a mistake. I thought perhaps there would be real writers here. Do you know Walker Percy? Or Thomas Pynchon? I thought I might be able to talk to someone like that. I'd sell my soul—if I had one—for a chance to spend an hour with a man like that. Instead they have Jim Phillips. And Phillip James."

"They're the same person," I said lamely.

"I know. God! They're *all* the same person. You and that fat woman over there and Elaine Westover and Carlton Gillespie and Leslie Hawes and Hamlyn Brent and Phillip James and Jim Phillips and—I." He stood up abruptly. "I've got to get a drink somewhere," he muttered, and left me sitting there. To pay for his coffee as well as mine.

When I went into the dining room at lunchtime, shortly

17

afterward, I didn't see a single person I knew—not even that awful sports coat hanging onto Van Saylor. So I didn't protest when the hostess put me with three other. women Writers who had come to the conference with their feminine briefcases bulging with their various efforts. One of them is Mrs. Annabel Strickland, from Atlanta, head of the Atlanta chapter of The Scribbling Club. She says. She's working on an absolutely certain best seller she won't discuss—much—because she's afraid somebody will steal her idea. All she *will* say—and at great length —is that it's about Thomas Jefferson and a lady friend of his who was "more than just a friend, if you know what I mean, dear." I didn't even tell her somebody has already stolen her idea.

Mrs. Strickland is about forty-five, and I'm afraid she must be hitting the menopause. She's small and intense and nearsighted, and sort of flustered and forgetful and perspiry, and she talks at random most of the time so that it's hard to follow her. She's also a little hard of hearing. I hope she doesn't think I want her book idea. She glares at me suspiciously whenever she thinks of the possibility. She dyes her hair a kind of weird bright brown with black walnut shells. She told me so. She has an herb garden that was her mother's, and she also makes dye out of all kinds of odd plants like joe-pye weed, whatever that is, and dyes her own clothes as well as her hair. And they look it. I'll bet she spun the thread and wove the cloth, too.

Then there's an overweight character, Mrs. Sophie Nelson, from a small town named Decibel, Alabama. She works on "the women's side," she says, of the *Decibel Weekly* and writes a column called "Sophie's Sidelights."

She had always felt a certain cameraderie with Carlton Gillespie, on account of *his* column. She wears too-short skirts as wide as they are long, and she always smells like bourbon and peppermint. She invited me, confidentially, to come up to her room any time I want a drink. "I know what writers are like," she says broadmindedly, winking with her mind's eye. She's writing a Biblical novel about Moses and his sister, but she says there isn't any incest in it. She's very fond of the Bible in a sort of unreligious way, she says; she reads it for fun.

The fourth woman at our table is Miss Marianna De-Brett, a ramrod type, head of the Women's Garden Club at Melrose, Alabama, and writing a book called *God's Garden.* She says it's Inspirational—she intends to get the Overflow from Dr. Norman Vincent Peale. She talks with upper-case emphasis all the time, which is exhausting to listen to.

After lunch I went to Mr. Hamlyn Brent's first mystery workshop. That was when he gave us the rules and the assignments and all. There are about twelve in the group, including Miss DeBrett, who says she's planning to Dash Off a Little Mystery in her spare time from Inspiration.

I don't really think any one of my three table companions had anything to do with the murder of Carlton Gillespie. But, as Miss DeBrett would say, they certainly are a trio of Unlikely Characters.

2

Monday Night

The picnic last night was one of Dean Crossett's little efforts to make the writers' conference seem like a vacation to the people from all over the state and nearby states who paid their tuition fees to attend. Students at the college get in at a reduced rate—that's how Dad can afford for me to be here. Once in a while my conscience tells me I shouldn't have even asked him—he works so hard at the store and hardly ever buys anything he wants for himself —but then I remember how proud he sounds when he tells some friend (while I squirm), "She's going to be a writer." Mother's even worse; she says, "Libby's a writer, you know," on the strength of a few bits and pieces in the college magazine. I tell myself that's why I've got to make this a great mystery novel, one that'll surely get published

—that it's for them. But really it's mostly for me. My ego is as appalling as Dory Pevlin's, only it doesn't show as much.

Anyway, Dad said the half price for tuition and board and all wasn't going to break him. But the Writers like Mrs. Nelson and Mrs. Strickland have to pay a hundred dollars for the week, as well as their hotel bills. So the Dean had lined up a barbecue, a banquet, a fish fry, a play by the Summer School Theater, and a musical evening, for the rest of the week's entertainment.

I went to the picnic about an hour early, just to be there in the Founders' Garden. I may as well admit I'm a romance freak, and I love the Founders' Garden. I mean, I did, before Mr. Gillespie got killed there and spoiled it. It's the most beautiful little walled garden, over at one side of the center. Actually the garden was there before the center, which they built on the site of the first college building that was the whole thing when it was started with twenty students back in the Dark Ages, long before the Foundation endowed it.

The garden has a high brick-lace wall, mossy with age, and inside it herb beds are laid out, surrounded by herringbone brick walks leading to a flowery terrace. The walks all radiate in a kind of spoke effect from a huge old millstone placed flat in the center, and between the bricks thyme is growing, smelling very herbish when crushed underfoot. There are old-fashioned pink and white roses blooming now, and the spice-bush with its long purple spikes that some people say is the original frankincense. There's a sundial, with the ominous foreshadowing on the base: *It is later than you think.* I love it all, and someday

I'm going to make myself a garden just like that. But without any millstone. I don't want to be reminded of Mr. Gillespie's dead body.

I thought I'd be alone there for about an hour, just peacefully smelling around like Ferdinand the Bull, before the picnic got started. But when I opened the wrought-iron gates and slipped inside, there was Mrs. Annabel Strickland futzing around in her dyed homespun dress (it was a kind of uncertain purple, "just the color of joe-pye-weed flowers," she had told me at lunch), waving her palm-leaf fan in front of her flushed and perspiring face.

"Hello," I said. "You got here early too?"

"What *is* this plant that smells like sage?" Mrs. Strickland held out a sprig to me.

"It *is* sage, Mrs. Strickland," I said politely.

"Oh." She smelled it again, doubtfully, as though things could not possibly ever be what they seemed, even to somebody who ought to know because she had an herb garden that was her mother's, at home. "I thought this picnic was to be at seven o'clock," she said petulantly, frowning at her watch accusingly.

"It is," I said. "And here comes somebody else." I wasn't to have my romantic hour alone in the garden at all. Not only Mrs. Strickland with her weeds and dyes and Tom Jefferson's amours, but Mrs. Nelson, with her whiskey and gin and Bible references, had waddled down to the garden early. I doubt if Mrs. Nelson ever knows whether it's morning or evening anyhow, the way she stays in a rosy haze that includes several kinds of liquor and all the personalities of the Old Testament. She really knows a mighty lot about the Bible, to be as vague as she is about

22

almost everything else. She knows a lot about drinks, too. She says gin is cheaper, but she does like Jack Daniel's better. So I guess that's some kind of whiskey. I'm not into liquor much; at The Butcher Shop we drink beer. And we don't have enough money for much of that.

Mrs. Nelson greeted us with a happy smile. "I enjoyed Dr. Petersen's lecture this afternoon so much!" she said. "He's giving me a personal conference tomorrow, and I hope he can straighten me out on plot. I've got everything but plot in *Moses and Miriam.* He says a novel really needs a plot. That hadn't occurred to me before, but I suppose he's right. Don't you think so, Annabel?"

"I've got a plot for *The Mistress,*" Mrs. Strickland said suspiciously, "but don't go asking me what it is, Sophie, because I'm not telling anybody. A friend of mine had a hundred-thousand word novel ready to go to a publisher, and the day she was going to mail it she read a review of a novel that had just come out, and it was her exact same plot and characters and all. I'm not risking anything like that happening."

"Aren't you even going to tell Dr. Petersen?" Mrs. Nelson was slurring her consonants, but only a little. "How can he give you all that good advice, then? Aren't you going to have a li'l ol' pers'nal conference with him about all your li'l ol' politicians and love stuff and all?"

"Of course not," Mrs. Strickland said, managing to look almost maidenly as well as embarrassed. "I couldn't talk to a *man* about the things that went on in those bedrooms in colonial times. The research was interesting, though. You know, I'll have to publish it under a *nom-de-plume.* I couldn't let anybody at home know I'd write

23

about things like that. Burdolph would just die. My husband," she explained.

"You mean we'll have to read *all* the novels about colonial times and guess which is yours?" Mrs. Nelson was struck by this as very funny, and went off into a high hysterical laughing jag.

"Well, it may not be published any time soon," Mrs. Strickland said modestly. "It's got to be as long as *Gone With The Wind,* and I've done only the first chapter so far. Just the scene where he first meets the girl. She has on her clothes in this one. It's at a tea dance. So I guess Dr. Petersen could see that much if he wants to."

"I don't think they had tea dances in colonial times," Mrs. Nelson said, but doubtfully, as became one whose period was purely Biblical.

"They do in my book," Mrs. Strickland said firmly. She had the omnipotent viewpoint, all right.

I saw Mel Alston strolling toward the garden gate with his mother, and I left the two novelists to it. I hoped Mel would introduce me to his mother. He's a tall handsome blond guy; I like him quite a lot, though I don't generally go out for football.

Mel did introduce us, and I sat with them on the wrought-iron benches and chatted for a while. June Gillespie is very well preserved, for a blonde, and she has an air of poise and self-possession that I can't help admiring. Even when she saw her husband come into the garden with Elaine Westover, she didn't turn a single sleek blond hair. But Mel scowled like crazy. Mrs. Gillespie smoothed out the frown on his forehead with her hand, playfully (almost warningly it was, I thought afterward, as though she were saying, "Don't let anyone know we care!") as she got up to go to meet them. "See you later," she said to us both in a casual, friendly tone. I saw her go and take her husband's arm, speaking to the red-lipped poetess just as casually. And I admired her still more. She wasn't so unperturbed about the whole thing later—but that was yet for me to find out.

"Your mother's quite a woman," I told Mel.

"Yes," he agreed, still frowning. Then he burst out as though he couldn't suppress it any longer, "He shouldn't be allowed to do that to her! I could kill that Elaine Westover! And—"

"Oh, it can't be anything serious," I soothed. "Your mother's a lot more attractive than Elaine Westover."

"I know," he said. "But he's *got* Mother. It makes him look such a fool, playing around. I never had much respect for him, but this—You don't know how serious it is," he added bitterly. "I came with her because—" He broke off that sentence and changed it to, "Mother might even have to divorce him."

"So what?" I said lightly. "Looks like you wouldn't mind that too much. Since you and your sister are both grown up, it wouldn't make a lot of difference, would it?"

"Carla's crazy about him, though," he muttered. "It's a wonder she'd go so far away from him as Radcliffe to go to college. I'd have gone as far away as I could get." He stood up and hesitated, looking down at me; then he broke a branch of the spice-bush and stripped it, savagely. The spiky fragrance was all around us. I got up, too, and took both his tense hands in mine, just to spare the poor Founders' Garden any more damage.

25

"Mel, Mel—" I murmured. Then, as it seemed obvious, "Why didn't you go somewhere else—up North, maybe?"

He let the spice-bush go and gripped my hands, and my fingers felt mashed because his were so strong. Then he noticed and relaxed his hold. "I'm sorry. I don't know why I should bother you with all this—"

"Because I'm nosy and I asked you." I tried again for the lighter touch. "Besides, what are friends for?"

He gave me an odd frowning look. "I could tell you anything, couldn't I? But I guess I don't really hate him for anything but hurting Mother. It's his money; he had a right to say he couldn't afford to send me to college anywhere but right here. Because he and the sports editor could get me a football scholarship here."

"I thought he made plenty of money, with all his various writings," I said, just for something to say. The Gillespies look well endowed.

"He does. But not for me. I'm not *his* son; he never lets me forget that. He never stops rubbing it in about every cent he ever spent on me, being so big-hearted as to bring up another man's son."

I felt very sorry for him; it must have been sad to grow up with a man like that around instead of a father like my dad. "Never mind," I said softly, taking my hands out of his but giving him a comforting pat or two. "After all, you're a senior. It won't be much longer."

"No," he said grimly. "It won't be much longer."

Those were words I couldn't help remembering later.

But at the time nobody would have suspected it was Carlton Gillespie's last supper, that fried chicken and potato salad and pickles and cake that Dean Crossett's boys from the dining hall were spreading on the long table they had brought and placed over against the wall back of the sundial. *It is later than you think,* the sundial's legend insisted ominously. But nobody in that cheerful group would have guessed it was so late for Carlton Gillespie.

The garden was filling up with Writers, now. It was eating time, and I was hungry. "Let's go get ourselves some food," I said to Mel.

"It's getting awfully crowded around here," he said, and his eyes were on the group around his stepfather and his mother and Miss Westover. If looks could have guillotined, the poetess's shapely head with its swirls of midnight hair and Carlton Gillespie's with its waxed eyebrows and mustache would both have fallen and rolled together into the basket, right then. "I think I'll skip the picnic. You don't mind, do you, Libby, if I don't stay? I don't believe I can stand to see—It makes me sick," he said frankly. "I'm going. But look, how about meeting me later tonight? After all this writing business is over and you're through with your mystery stuff—?"

"Well, all right," I said. "But it may be late. There's no formal workshop or lecture scheduled for tonight, but they might have what they call an informal get-together, I heard. Want to meet me here in the garden? It smells wonderful here when the night-blooming jasmine opens. It's a very romantic spot."

"Good," he said, but absently; football players aren't what I call romantic, even when they're sexy like Mel.

"Okay. 'Bye, then."

He left me as quickly as though he really were sick, and again I was sorry for him. I hadn't known before that football stars ever took anything to heart but the pigskin.

I filled a plate at the table, took my glass of iced Russian tea in my other hand (for some reason people around this college consider tea steeped with orange peel and spices sophisticated and call it Russian—White Russian, of course), and headed back for the bench I had been sitting on. Twilight had fallen now and the shadows of the shrubbery half hid the bench. Until I was practically sitting down in his lap I didn't realize that the cadaverous man with the beard, Jim Phillips, was now occupying it. He sat with his paper plate beside him, not eating, just watching the others eat, with a kind of hungry expression, as if he had ulcers.

"Mind if I sit with you?" I asked brightly.

He smiled sort of remotely (and he didn't look so all-gone when he smiled), moving the plate to give me room. "Please do."

"I'm Libby Clark. I'm here for the mystery workshop. I know you, of course, Mr. Phillips," I said, unconsciously choosing his pen name that was on *The Horizontal Streaker* instead of the religious-magazine one. I went on burbling, "Are you an Alabama man, Mr. Phillips? They seem to be specializing in Alabama writers here."

"I lived here some years ago," he said politely. "That may be why they invited me to talk—as an Alabama writer. But I'm living in Florida now."

"I hope to hear your talk tomorrow," I offered, being just as polite. I did, too. I was curious about how he did his split-personality bit, going from religion to streaker.

"You should," he said abruptly, almost savagely. "I'm going to tell them not to write the way I do. I write just for the money, you know."

"What else is there?" I said flippantly. I didn't really feel the way I sounded. I didn't mean to set him off on a flashback.

"I was going to write such magnificent things," he said broodingly. "Things that would lift American prose to new heights—"

It sounded pompous and silly to me. "Eat your fried chicken," I said soothingly, taking a bite out of my drumstick and following it with a forkful of potato salad. I seemed to be soothing every man I spoke to. He obeyed almost automatically, as though he needed someone to tell him what to do. So he's that kind of man, I thought. Dependent on some woman, helpless without her. He wasn't the least bit attractive—no more than Van Saylor and just as old—but he interested me. I wanted to explore why he had turned against writing for money. That seemed like a pretty good objective to me. He seemed to have more depth than Mr. Saylor, anyway. And he didn't wear a plaid sports coat. His suit was dark and a bit worn at the cuffs of sleeves and trousers.

"That's right. It's good chicken, isn't it?" I said. "Not bad potato salad, either."

The plastic fork wasn't a very secure implement; it wavered in his hand and dropped some potato salad on his beard. Embarrassed, he dabbed at it with his paper napkin and almost got it all.

I said hurriedly, as if I didn't notice, "Well, why is it you don't write what you want to? If you're unhappy about things like *The Horizontal Streaker?*"

"I've got to have money to get my daughter Dale through college." He sat scowling at his inmost soul for a minute and threw his drumstick bone at an innocent toad that hopped near his foot. "She's at Radcliffe." He took a long drink of tea and wiped his beard again with the paper napkin, which was almost in shreds by now. Every fried chicken picnic plate should be served with at least three napkins. "Publishers don't want the kind of things I need to write, to satisfy myself. All they want from me is stuff like my next assignment, a gory little thing called *Murder in the Clover.* It'll probably be banned to keep adolescents from using it for a do-it-yourself handbook. But they'll give me a two-thousand advance. And I can pay Dale's tuition next semester. Fortunately she doesn't use my pen name. Her friends don't have to know—"

"Radcliffe." I made conversation, trying to divert him. "That's where Mr. Gillespie's daughter Carla goes, too, Mel was telling me. He's her half-brother, you know."

"Yes. If I write as many as four of those stinking things this year, Dale can have as many clothes and as much spending money as Carla Gillespie. Maybe I'll have to write only three if I do reams of that insipid religious stuff too."

"Oh, money's not everything," I said. "Maybe Dale isn't as extravagant as you think. Maybe if she knew you want to write a really great novel, she'd help. Do with less."

"She hasn't had a chance to develop any—any affection for me," he said, and I thought his voice sounded very sad. "We don't know each other very well. Her grandmother brought her up after her mother died. They say Gillespie's daughter is crazy about him. You see pictures of them together—" he added wistfully.

"Well, all you have to do is get to know her," I said briskly, and I wondered for a brief self-questioning instant if my father felt we know each other well enough. But I know we do, Dad and I. "It must be your own fault if you don't make the effort—"

"It is. It is!" he said—savagely again. "But—it's not all my fault. The blame is easy to share."

"Eat your supper," I said again, because I get uneasy with these temperamental, excitable writers. He started eating the salad as if it had no taste at all, and I saw with relief that Mrs. Sophie Nelson was bearing down on us like a vast rolling stone in a printed-silk pants suit with matching tote bag, carrying a glass but no plate.

"What are you lurking here in the dark for, where nobody can see you?" she said loudly, laughing her booming laugh.

"The bench is too heavy to move, anchored in concrete this way," I explained frivolously, ignoring her arch suggestion. "Have you met Mr. Phillips, Mrs. Nelson?"

He stood up briefly; she waved him back to his seat. "I won't sit down," she assured him, and she probably meant it at the moment. "But don't you two want a little bitty drop of something else in those glasses? I've been adding plenty to mine—it tastes impossible without it. Tastes— would you believe it?—like tea with orange peel in it. Here —" She pulled a flat bottle out of her flowered bag and held it out. "Plenty left. Have some."

I put my hand up to stop her, but she had already poured about a half jigger into my Russian tea. Well, I could pour it out later. Mr. Phillips said brusquely, "No, thanks."

"Come now, Mr. Phillips. Don't tell me you don't drink. All writers drink. All those orgies in your books—you couldn't have made up such ver—veris'militude—"

"I was a drunk once," he said with what sounded like rough self-contempt. "When I decided to make my comeback—into the smooth rarefied air of paperback books and religious magazines—I went into a sanitarium."

Sophie apparently had a mental block against any kind of drying-out health farm. "You haven't got TB too, as well as being on the wagon?" She seemed genuinely horrified at his sufferings.

"That I have had too," he admitted. "But that wasn't the kind of sanitarium I meant. Have you ever had delirium tremens, Mrs. Nelson?"

"Man, you need a drink if anybody does," she urged sympathetically. But she hadn't answered his pertinent question. Or did she consider it impertinent?

He shook his head again.

I had had enough.

"Here, you sit down, Mrs. Nelson," I said. "I see Mr. Hawes over there, and I want to ask him something. You tell Mr. Phillips about *Moses and Miriam*. He can give you some pointers about plot." And I unmercifully left him caught, with the eager Sophie starting to give him the lowdown on life in the days of the Pentateuch.

I didn't really want to see Mr. Hawes about anything, but as I took my empty plate and spiked glass back to the table and received in return a smaller plate of vanilla ice cream and fudge cake and started away, he smiled at me and said, "Miss Clark, come and meet my wife."

"I'd like to," I said warmly, because I liked Mr. Hawes

in spite of those heavy-handed historical novels. "Hi, Mrs. Hawes."

"Hello, Miss Clark." She smiled, too, and I thought she must have been very pretty as a girl. She isn't old now, of course, but she looks a bit worn and worried around the eyes. They say three children can do that to you. Her brown hair isn't done, just combed, as though there were never enough time. She looks like a typical younger-faculty wife, trying to make his salary go around by wearing the same clothes she wore last time she went anywhere.

"Why, you really are beautiful!" she said to me, as though it surprised her. "You look like a gypsy—a beautiful dark gypsy with red under the tan of your cheeks. I take it all back, Leslie—" Well, I had to like her, after that. She could see I didn't know what she was talking about, so she laughed and explained. "He told me he had made Rinda, the heroine of the book he's working on, look like one of his students named Libby Clark, because she's so lovely. I said it didn't sound convincing—that nobody could be as beautiful as he made Rinda."

"Well, thanks," I murmured inadequately. "I'll be sure to read about her when the book comes out." I was embarrassed and changed the subject. "Do you write too, Mrs. Hawes?"

"Oh, I was a reporter once." She smiled. "And I used to write poetry, a long time ago. But you get over that."

"Here come Mr. and Mrs. Gillespie," Mr. Hawes said. "Have you met them? I did last night at the staff party."

I shook my head, saying, "Only Mrs. Gillespie," and Mrs. Hawes said, "Yes, I know Carlton. He and I worked on the paper together in Birmingham, you know, Leslie, a long time ago."

"Oh, I remember, so you did." He was greeting the Gillespies now and introducing us. "This is my wife, Kay, Mrs. Gillespie. I believe you know Miss Clark. Miss Clark, Mr. Gillespie. Kay tells me you and she are old friends," he said genially to Mr. Gillespie. "That she used to work on the paper with you."

"Oh, yes, we certainly are." Carlton Gillespie acknowledged it with a sort of questioning glance at Mrs. Hawes. I wondered if they had gone together when they worked on the paper. She had flushed a bit; she didn't look too happy about meeting him again.

Mr. Hawes pursued cordially, "If you have time while you're here, you must come out to the house and meet the family."

"Yes, do," Kay said, lifting her head and looking straight into Carlton Gillespie's eyes. "You'd like the boys. The oldest one is nearly ten."

If I weren't in training to be a writer I might not have been so observant, watching every glance and tone of voice. But later I was glad I was.

Mrs. Gillespie said, "We'd like to, of course, but they have so much planned for us to do here. But maybe—"

Mr. Gillespie said, with a neat and quite unconvincing appearance of being sorry, "If only I didn't have to correct those galleys and get them back to Jack! It means I have to be working most of my spare time, and there's really *no* spare time—"

"You know about his new book?" June Gillespie said proudly to the Haweses. "His first big hardcover novel!

He's had a number of them in the slick magazines, of course, but this is a serious one he's been working on for nearly ten years. It's sure to be a best seller. It might even win him the Pulitzer to add to his Forrester Prize."

"What is it called?" Mr. Hawes asked politely. After all, he had published several hardcover novels. But none of them had been best sellers or won any prizes.

"It's called *The Passionate Circumstance*," Mrs. Gillespie advertised, as a good public-relations-type wife should, smiling at her husband, who looked uncomfortable. "The title is from a wonderful poem of his, printed in the front—" And she quoted, right there to all of us,

> *"Come, cross the passionate circumstance!*
> *There is no truth till that be done;*
> *Till the hot hearts come pantingly*
> *From the green courses where they run,*
> *And lie down under some green tree*
> *—With blood as quick in every sense—*
> *And learn to await indifferently*
> *The hazards of experience."*

She looked around triumphantly, and I followed her glance. Mr. Gillespie was looking even more uncomfortable, obviously sorry that his ego had led him to mention the proofs, Mr. Hawes was saying with vague goodwill, "Well, that ought to sell it, all right," and I went on eating my ice cream. I nearly dropped the plate, though, when I noticed that Mrs. Hawes had turned white and was staring at Mr. Gillespie as though she couldn't quite take in what she realized must be so. Someone turned on the garden's few artistically effective spotlights just then, and the white glare might have accounted for her pallor. But her eyes blazed and her lips were thin with scorn.

Mr. Hawes didn't notice anything, but I think Mrs. Gillespie did. Mr. Hawes asked courteously into the stiff silence, "And what is the novel about?"

"It's about a young man's realization that he is a man," June Gillespie explained. "Its setting is a newspaper, of course—it's the setting Carlton knows best. Mostly about the hero's affair with a woman reporter—how they loved each other so violently, and then she let herself get pregnant and he had to leave her in order to be true to himself and his destiny—oh, it has all the best-seller elements. It uses utterly frank language, of course, but I think today's critics will applaud that. There are some scenes that—well, I never worked on the paper, or they might think I was the woman. Of course they'll say Carlton's done an autobiographical novel—but it's fiction, I can guarantee that. We'd been married nine years at that time. But everybody in Birmingham will be trying to identify the girl. You tell me if you recognize her, Kay, when you read the book." She laughed and hugged her husband's arm.

"I certainly would like to read it," Mrs. Hawes said slowly, and her voice was as tense as her face. "May I read the proofs, Carlton?"

"Why—Why—" he stammered, "I don't think there'll be time, Kay, though I certainly would like to have your opinion. You see, I have to get them right back to the publisher—there's a deadline to meet—"

"I'd like to see those proofs, Carlton," she repeated, and it wasn't just a polite request. It was a breathless pressure.

"I might recognize the woman, at that. And—so might a good many other people. You might reconsider publishing it, to avoid ruining someone's life. Maybe a child's. But that would be nothing to you if you could win a prize, as you did—" There was furious contempt in her voice.

"Look here, Kay," Mr. Hawes said bewilderedly, "what are you talking about? Mrs. Gillespie'll think—"

"Yes," June Gillespie said. "She will." They had all quite forgotten I was there. I had moved a little bit back into the shadows.

"You don't mean—" Mr. Hawes got it at last. "No—Kay—"

"I don't keep any secrets from my husband," Mrs. Hawes said with a certain significance to Mr. Gillespie. "Except—once—a name."

Carlton Gillespie was looking less debonair every minute. I wondered objectively if *The Passionate Circumstance* would ever be published. Mr. Hawes was much bigger than Mr. Gillespie, I noted rather gladly. The girl reporter's careless pregnancy *had* to tie up with Kay's early remark to Mr. Gillespie about seeing her oldest son. It was strange—but good—if she really had no secrets from her husband.

But they all seemed like such regular, ordinary people. Ordinary people do have weird things seething around in the hidden parts of their lives, I thought with a kind of excitement that I was a little bit ashamed of. Because I liked Professor Hawes and his wife, and I liked Mel's mother, and they seemed to be going to get it in the neck, all of them. Because of Mr. Gillespie.

"It's time we went back to the center," Gillespie said to

his wife, his voice touched with desperation, it seemed to me.

"To get the proofs to show me?" Mrs. Hawes said relentlessly. "We'll come too, won't we, Leslie?"

I murmured, "Excuse me—" and faded out, but they didn't even hear me or see me; they hadn't for some time. Mr. Gillespie took his wife by the arm and started away from Mr. and Mrs. Hawes. They escaped while the Professor was trying to keep his wife from following them, arguing with her to wait and calm down and tell him all about it and then they'd see what should be done.

"You know what he's done," I could hear her say in that low furious voice. "The skunk has made a novel out of it all—and used my poem for the title!—so that everybody who ever knew me—Nobody but you knew about it *all.* And he's probably added to it, too. Made it seem even worse than it was—and it was bad enough. Such a fool I was. Oh, Leslie, what it will do to you here at the college —probably stop your promotion—and the children—"

"You didn't tell me—who the man was," he said, his jaw tight. "But don't get so upset now, Kay," he begged, trying to be kind to her. "It probably won't be a best seller at all. He's not a very good writer, in my opinion. Probably nobody will even read it."

"It'll sell in Alabama, all right," she said bitterly. "Everybody here will read it. All right, let's go home."

They moved off, and as they passed a light I saw her face. It was something to remember.

But she doesn't look strong enough to have killed Carlton Gillespie the way he was killed. Mr. Hawes does. I wonder if he went over and made Mr. Gillespie show him the proofs later on last night?

I speculated about how Mr. Phillips and Mrs. Nelson were getting along, on their obscure bench out of sight of the crowd (she's a grass widow, she says, not sod), but I didn't want to get involved with them again. Then I saw Mrs. Nelson with Mrs. Strickland, and realized he must have managed to get away.

Well, I could dodge them. I would go back to the center. It was about nine o'clock, and the picnic was looking frazzled around the edges by now anyway.

3

Monday Night and Tuesday Dawn

I stopped by the desk to speak to the desk clerk, a casual friend of mine named Frank Benton, who's a part-time student here in his spare time. Just out of curiosity I asked, "Say, Frank, what room are the Gillespies in?" I thought if they were on my floor, I might notice if the Professor and Mrs. Hawes came by later on to see those very interesting proofs.

"They're in three-forty-seven," he said. "Right next to Miss Westover. Real handy."

"Oh, really, Frank," I protested. "You know they'd have better sense than that. Who arranged it that way, anyhow?" I couldn't help asking. "Did he mention it? Or she?"

"I did it myself," he said modestly. "Just call me Cupid

Benton. Naturally the management of the center wants everybody to have a good time at this (deleted) conference. Can I fix you up any special way?"

"I'm fixed," I told him. "Why don't you fix that so-called (deleted) self-service elevator if you want to fix something? Half the time the door won't close and it won't move, and I have to walk up to the third floor."

"You just don't know how to handle it," Frank said. "You have to cuss at it. You should hear Dean Crossett get it going," he added admiringly. "He never repeats himself. He doesn't delete anything, either. He does it very softly, almost in a whisper, but it works. The door eventually closes. After he kicks it for a while, too."

"I'll walk," I said resignedly.

When I found out the air conditioning in my room wouldn't work, I wished I had stayed in the garden, even though it had too many people still in it. I thought, I'll call Frank and see if there's a chance of somebody fixing it tonight. Or at least get some ice. That is, if the phone works.

I must have been psychic. There *was* something wrong with the phone. The lines were crossed. When I picked up my receiver I heard a man's voice saying, "You'll have to get the money or do the job, that's all." I thought, Surely I must have Mr. Gillespie too much on my mind. I couldn't think of any other voice but his. That's the voice it sounded like.

The answer was just a hoarse sound of anger—or maybe despair. The smooth voice went on. "You know I loaned it to you with the understanding that you'd pay it back in a month. That was a year ago. I need it now. Yes, I know

41

you've been working for me, but only because I insisted. And you haven't come across with this latest job."

"Blackmail—" the hoarse voice ground out.

"Not a bit of it. I can use my money. You owe it to me. That's all. Just get it back to me. Or—do that other piece of work." The line went dead, and I couldn't rouse anybody when I tried again to get the desk.

Now what was all that about? Mr. Gillespie, if it was he, was bothering somebody about owing him money. He was making the other guy work for him, too. Work? What kind of work? Secretary? Typist? Which one of the men at the conference would fit that role? "That other piece of work"? That sounded sort of sinister, the Mafia or something like that. I pondered as I showered, and I couldn't decide on any answer to the puzzle. Oh, well, it wasn't any of my business anyhow, I told myself. I wasn't writing *The Mystery Book Mystery* then. Later, of course, I tried with all my mental ear power to identify the hoarse voice. But it was no use. The man had been so choked up with anger or whatever that it disguised his voice completely. The detective could hardly believe it when I told him. He thought I was fantasizing, or trying to shield someone. But I wasn't. I just don't know whose voice it was, that's all. I wish I did.

I lay down on the bed and tried to relax, but my mind ran on and on in lively speculations about Mrs. Hawes and Carlton Gillespie. If *The Passionate Circumstance* ever comes out, they can sure put me down for a copy. I won't even wait for the paperback edition.

The phone conversation was provocative, too. This writers' conference isn't going to be so dull after all, I thought happily as I got up to dress and meet Mel. I put on my thin yellow cotton, and white sandals. It was just possible that he would notice what I was wearing, though not likely. There was a half-moon blooming in that garden along with the night-scented stocks and white jasmine.

It was still early for my date—only a little after ten—when I went downstairs. There in the lobby I saw Jim Phillips standing over the long table, gazing down at *The Horizontal Streaker* and *Now I Lay Me Down*. His look was so unforgiving that I thought he might tear them apart with his hands, the way the Strong Man does the thick telephone book. I spoke to him as I passed, but he was brooding so over his brain children that he didn't even see me. When I glanced back at him he was sort of wiping his big hand over his face as if to banish his own disgust from his features. He walked over to the desk to talk to Frank Benton, and I drifted into the coffee shop. I was just in time to see the fight.

"What's going on?" I murmured to Mrs. Strickland, who sat settled for the evening in a sheltered corner behind a display of magazines, fanning herself vigorously and drinking hot coffee. Just to see her made you think, "What's wrong with this picture?" Mrs. Nelson sat with her, sipping on a glass of something-on-the-rocks. She had put the something on the rocks herself, of course. The coffee shop doesn't serve any but soft drinks. They're selling Mrs. Nelson many a glass of ice, though, during this conference.

"What's going on?" Mrs. Nelson answered instead of Mrs. Strickland. "Why, they're starting a real nice knock-down-and-drag-out fight, that's all, honey."

"That boy is drunk," Mrs. Strickland stated positively. I saw Dory Pevlin's face then, and I knew she was right. Dory was quite drunk. Unless he was stoned on hash or something worse. Belligerent drunk.

Carlton Gillespie had turned his back on Dory, where they both stood at the counter among the others waiting to be served. As I watched, Dory reached out and spun Mr. Gillespie by the shoulders around to face him again.

"I ought to kill you," Dory said.

He leaned forward, or maybe fell against Mr. Gillespie, and caught him again by the shoulders and shook him the way a dog shakes another dog when he has him by the throat, with blind, battling rage.

Mr. Gillespie was smaller than Dory and obviously not a fighting man. "Help—" he gasped out frantically toward Hamlyn Brent and several others who stood near. "Brent —stop this crazy idiot—"

Mr. Brent moved forward without visible enthusiasm, but at the same time Dean Crossett appeared with his authority showing and took Dory by the arm. "What do you mean by such an unwarranted attack on a college guest, young man?" he demanded. "You must know you can't jump on a man with no reason—"

"I've got a reason," Dory said. "I don't like him."

"You go on up to bed," Dean Crossett advised in his best fatherly manner that he used on unruly undergraduates rather effectively. "And tomorrow you apologize to Mr. Gillespie."

"Like hell I will," Dory said with emphasis.

"Now, Mr. Pevlin—" the Dean protested. Undergraduates don't talk back.

"You wouldn't like him either," Dory snarled. "I worked for two years in Birmingham to get my one-man show put on at The Gallery, and when they finally put it on, 'Gil's Day' was clever and sarcastic about it. So nasty and satiric and clever that it killed the whole thing. Now he comes along patronizing me, asking me when I'm going to have another show—and he knows I'll never get another show—he knows I haven't painted since—"

He was almost sobbing, with his anger and frustration released by whatever it was he was high on. It was a pitiful, embarrassing exhibition, and I was glad when the Dean gestured to Larry Mims to help him, and they each put a firm arm around Dory and succeeded in forcing him to come away with them. But as he hung back he muttered, "Apologize! I ought to kill him—he murdered an artist—" The Dean murmured tranquilizing words as they went, like vocal Miltowns.

Carlton Gillespie shook his clothes back into place, shrugged his slight shoulders tolerantly, as if to say drunks-will-be-drunks-but-thank-God-you-and-I-would-never-get-into-such-a-disgraceful-condition, and ordered iced coffee.

Frank Benton came in and called over the hubbub, "Mr. Brent! Could I see you a minute?"

I went on down to the garden to meet Mel Alston.

The garden was just lovely that night, before anything ugly happened there. The hired help had cleaned up all traces of the picnic, and the lights were turned off at ten-thirty so that the moonlight could show. There was a soft transparent whiteness over the open places, like a very

45

light frost, and the dark, shadowy clusters of trees and bushes were the darker for it. The air had that sweet, hot, dry smell that the sun had drawn from the summer flowers and left lingering there. When Mel was late—when eleven-thirty became ten minutes ago—I didn't care, at first, because it was so pleasant to be there in the garden alone.

But it's against my principles to wait longer than ten minutes for any date, and I couldn't make an exception even for a sexy football captain. I strolled toward the gate, and as I passed the clump of Japanese quinces in the darkest corner of the garden, I had the weird feeling that somebody was there. The feeling hadn't been there when I came in. Could somebody have slipped in while I was looking the other way? Obviously someone could.

I felt like running, not walking, to the gate. It couldn't be Mel, of course, I thought—why would he be hiding from me? We were too old for hide-and-seek. But I called out, "Mel?" just to be sure. And heard the quaver in my voice and knew I was frightened. All at once I was running toward the gate—with nobody at all after me. I felt utterly foolish when I saw somebody coming toward me. Mel at last?

No, it wasn't Mel. Somebody else with a late date in the garden, then?

It figured, all right. Because when he came near me I saw that it was Carlton Gillespie. And I wondered whether it was Elaine Westover—or maybe some other woman?—who had been waiting there in the dark, hoping I would go away before he came. Casanova Gillespie, I thought disdainfully. *Old* Casanova Gillespie. At least fifty.

I spoke to him as I passed him on the walk leading back to the center, and he smiled briefly with a glint of his teeth under that devilish mustache as he said, "Good night." It's kind of awe-making to realize that that might have been the last smile of Carlton Gillespie's life. I don't think he smiled as he met the person who was waiting for him. I admit I may have lingered a moment beside the wall, curious about which woman was there. Then I doubted that it *was* a date when I heard Mr. Gillespie say with rather a lot of astonishment in his voice, "So it's *you!* I *thought—*"

Reluctantly I stopped eavesdropping then and walked on, because he would have noticed if I hadn't. So I didn't hear the answer. Later that detective, Dopey Ayres, tried to make me have heard it. But if you didn't, you just didn't. I couldn't be a bit of help to him there. By that time I had already helped him quite a lot, and it seems to me he ought to be more grateful. Nobody else had noticed nearly as much as I had, and I didn't tell him everything *I'd* noticed. Because I wanted to see how the police went about finding out things like what Mrs. Hawes had said to Mr. Gillespie, and I wasn't going to get her in trouble if I could help it.

I went straight back to the center and to my room, not even glancing into the coffee shop to see who was there, because I wanted to be in if Mel should phone to apologize abjectly for oversleeping after supper or something. I even waited half an hour before undressing, getting more and more provoked with Mel. Then I decided it would be cooler to think nothing of it and perhaps make him wait a while for another date. He wasn't important enough to me—yet—to matter, and football players are just swarming everywhere in term time. I was already in bed when the phone rang at last.

It was Mel, and he *was* abject—just crawling. He hadn't meant to stand me up, he explained; he wouldn't have missed coming if he could have helped it, but just as he was starting to go and meet me, his mother phoned him at the frat house, sounding hysterical, talking about killing herself or *him* or That Woman, and he thought he ought to come by the center and see what was the matter and calm her down.

It turned out that, after coming upstairs from his encounter with Dory in the coffee shop, Mr. Gillespie had gone out again and refused maddeningly to tell his wife why, or whom he had a date with. All he would say was that she ought to get her mind above such suspicions, that it wasn't a woman, just a writing conference, and that she had no business suspecting him of fooling around anyway —that he had given all that up long ago. Mrs. Gillespie cried, said she wasn't blind and wasn't a bit deceived by his declaration. She begged him not to go—said he wouldn't if he had any love for her left—and he went anyway. So she went to pieces. When those calm, sophisticated ones break, they really shatter, I thought. Mel had just now managed to get her to bed, he said, and he had taken all her sleeping pills and Carlton Gillespie's toy pistol away with him, so he thought she couldn't do anything desperate tonight. He hadn't even gone to the garden, he said—he had known it was too late for me to be still waiting for him. He had just called me, while he was here at the center, to apologize. "I don't suppose you want to see me now?" he suggested, but not even hopefully. "I'll buy you a Coke—" He sounded still upset and unlike himself. His mother must have given him a really hard time.

"No, thanks," I told him. "I understand, and it's all right, Mel. But I'm in bed. Some other time. Good night."

"Good night, then. See you tomorrow." And I thought, with some indignation, that he even sounded relieved that I wouldn't meet him right then.

I was just turning over to try to go back to sleep when I heard someone come into the next room. Nothing special about the sounds—just an entering and a moving around, ordinary sounds. But it reminded me—in some instinct of self-preservation, I suppose—that I had forgotten to try the door between the two rooms to be sure it was locked. I guess there was some remnant of apprehension left over from that frightened feeling I had momentarily had in the garden. And my mother had brainwashed me into always being sure the connecting doors in hotel and motel rooms were locked; it was usually the first thing I did in a place like this, after I put down my bag and looked to see if there were waterbugs in the shower. How could I have forgotten this time?

I got up cautiously, snapping on the bed-table light. How could I try turning the doorknob without the occupant of the next room noticing? If I didn't try it before latching it, I might not be turning the latch the right way; I might be unlocking it instead of locking it.

Then I heard the water running in the bathroom next door. The walls are quite thin in this old building; you can hear almost everything that goes on next door. He must be in the bathroom; that's the shower, I surmised. So I could hurry and try the door before he came back into the room.

It *was* unlocked. My stealthy turning of the doorknob and the slight crack in the door went unnoticed, though. I guess he had to be in the shower, as I had imagined. I didn't stop to look. I just hastily turned the little latch that locked the door from my side, and wished there were a more substantial-looking lock. Evidently the two rooms were part of a suite if anybody should ever want a suite (but why would they?) in this center. I considered a moment and then pushed the largest armchair over in front of the door. At least I could hear it scrape if the door should be opened. I was glad I'm a light sleeper.

I went back to bed and turned off the light and lay there wondering why I should feel so tense and keyed-up. With hindsight, of course—*now*—it's simple to think that murder was in the air, that the molecules of the air carried the news to the molecules of my nervous system, the uneasy feeling that Death had been in the garden and that there were all sorts of electrical cross-currents in the violent feelings of the people concerned.

But *then* I thought it was just the potato salad, and I got up again and chewed a soda-mint, turned off the light, and lay down and shut my eyes firmly. After a while I slept, by simple will-power, but fitfully, with odd but unrememberable dreams. I woke up again at dawn and couldn't get back to sleep. I tossed around on the hot sheets for a while, thinking what a scorcher of a day was coming up. Then I decided I might as well get up and take a walk. Maybe go down to the garden and see if the tryst I had surprised there last night had left any traces.

Sure, I have a large element of curiosity. It's a good thing for a writer to have, I think. Besides, I've always liked the garden in the early morning, as well as at dusk and after dark. Dew on the thyme makes it smell even more delicious when your foot crushes it. I've often come down there before breakfast, from the dorm where I live in the regular semesters. It's only a short walk along the campus paths. And I have unrestricted curfew, so Mr. Bridgewater never wonders whether I'm coming in or going out. I'm glad Mother is a liberated woman; without a qualm, she signed for me to have unrestricted curfew and to live in an open dorm. Dad just trusts me—but Mother seems to rejoice in my freedom. It's so different from her college days.

From the center it took an even shorter time to get to the garden. I saw the sun coming up, and it looked white and hot already. A few drops of dew still glittered on the spider webs and grass blades, but it was rapidly drying off. The wrought-iron gate into the garden was ajar. Usually Mr. Bridgewater or the other campus security guard closes it on his last round, about ten-thirty. But it's never locked. Of course, I thought, Mr. Gillespie and the person he met forgot to close it when they came out last night. I went inside, and the gate made a clanging noise as it swung shut behind me.

The noise seemed as though it must startle the deep silence that lay over the garden. This lack of sound was almost unnatural, I was faintly aware; not a bird spoke.

Then I saw the source of the silence. I saw Carlton Gillespie lying in that awful bloody mess on the millstone, and I was so shocked I couldn't even scream. I stood there with my eyes shut trying not to see him, for *such* a long time—my heart staggering along in loud thumps, a roaring in my ears; I clung to a tree so I wouldn't fall down if I fainted. After a while I knew I had to open my eyes again. I had to go and look at him, in case he might be still alive, so that something could be done to help him. But somehow I knew with awful certainty that he wasn't still alive.

I managed to make myself go to him. You have to experience everything to be a writer, I told myself. Newspaper reporters have to look at dead bodies. Probably Kay Hawes, when she was a reporter . . . I realized that my mind was trying to escape, going off at tangents to keep from focusing on Carlton Gillespie.

After I forced myself to take a good look at his face, I had no doubt that he was dead. It was the *fixed* look of his features, I think, and the fixed look of his sprawled limbs. You knew, to look at his face and his body, that they could never be mobile again. His jaunty eyebrows and mustache and beard looked awfully out of place, as though glued onto that livid flesh as some macabre joker's afterthought.

Nevertheless, I leaned over him, feeling sick at my stomach, but thinking vaguely that I ought to feel for his pulse. With gingerly fingers I touched his wrist. I couldn't feel any flutter, but I hadn't expected to. I realized then that I didn't actually know how to feel a pulse. And for some reason—probably that I was still dazed with shock —I hadn't noticed until this minute that the watch on his wrist had been smashed, probably by hitting the edge of the brick curb as he fell. I knew from all my background mystery-book reading what this meant. It was one way the police could know the time he was killed.

Sternly urging myself, I turned the still wrist over, to look at the face of the watch. It had stopped, sure enough.

At 12:05. Just about fifteen minutes after I had seen him at the gate.

4

Tuesday Morning

What are you doing here? I asked myself. Why don't you go and get somebody? Then I caught sight of the little piece of black printing on thin paper that lay lightly on the dead man's breast, pinned there with a single straight pin. It had obviously been put there after the violence that strangled him and smashed the back of his head in. A flutter would have moved it, but there was no flutter, only that dreadful stillness.

I did not dare touch it; I knew one must not ever touch anything at the scene of the crime. But I could read it without touching. It seemed to be a familiar type of printing, and after a puzzled moment I realized where I had seen such print. In Bibles, of course. It was a small bit cut out neatly and laminated between two pieces of cellophane tape. And I read it aloud to myself, there in the garden where murder had been: "No man shall take the nether or the upper millstone to pledge, for he taketh a man's life to pledge."

What in the world did it mean? For a moment I was so interested that I forgot to feel so terribly sick; I even forgot to keep swallowing hard. There must be some reason why that particular Bible verse was left when Carlton Gillespie was—the word "executed" came to my mind. No. Of course he wasn't executed. But perhaps he had been punished for some sufficient sin. . . .

I stood up and moved toward the gate, trying to feel only a detached horror instead of a personal nausea. I'm sure I would have felt much worse if the dead man had been somebody I really knew. But I had met him only yesterday—though I had been reading him for years—and I hadn't liked him much when I *did* meet him. So it was possible, I analyzed, for me to regard his dead body rather as a piece of literary property than as something to get hysterical about. Still, I wasn't exactly calm. Frank Benton told me that I looked like a drunk ghost when I came weaving into the lobby and told him Carlton Gillespie had been murdered in the garden, and to call Mr. Bridgewater or somebody.

"How do you know?" he said skeptically. He couldn't have thought I was walking in my sleep and having a nightmare. But then it was the first time there had ever been a murder at the college, and I don't much blame Frank for not being able to take it in, just at first.

"How do I know? Because he's dead—and he couldn't have committed suicide by smashing the back of his head against the millstone."

"Maybe he fell, maybe it was an accident," Frank suggested.

"You go look at him. It was no accident. He'd have had to fall a dozen times to beat his head in like that. Besides, he looks as if he were choked to death too."

"What are we standing here talking for?" Frank grabbed the phone. He called Mr. Bridgewater's number —he lives at Mrs. Gussey's boarding house just off the campus in back of the library—and told him to get down to the garden quick. Then he called the police department in town, telling them (with no skepticism at all now— rather with incoherent excitement) what I had told him. Then he rushed out to the garden to see for himself.

I went on up to my room—and I had to walk those three flights of stairs on my shaky legs; the elevator wouldn't move. I lay down on the bed; I felt weak and not much like a mystery writer. I wasn't inured to corpses anywhere but on paper.

For the first time—in the excitement it hadn't crossed my mind before—it struck me to wonder who had killed Mr. Gillespie. And as I thought about it, I realized that a good many people would fit pretty well as suspects. There were a number of folks around who rather violently didn't like him. Mrs. Hawes—but no woman could have done that particular murder unless she was a professional at killing. And stronger than *she* looks. Professor Hawes, then, because of Mrs. Hawes. And—Mel, because of his mother and because of his long resentment of his stepfather. And Dory Pevlin, who had been so drunk and angry and who had actually said, "I ought to kill you," to Carlton Gillespie. And—what about the man on the phone?

The mystery writers' handbook said money was frequently a motive for murder. Gillespie was demanding the return of money from someone who didn't have it, and had some onerous hold on the other man.

That made four people at least—not counting the women—who might have wished he were dead. But they wouldn't . . . surely people didn't kill other people . . . not people I knew . . . not Mel Alston? But he *had* failed to keep his date with me in the garden, and he had sounded mighty upset and disturbed when he called me—and it *was* after 12:05. That story about his mother wasn't one the detectives would accept for an alibi if they ever found out Mrs. Gillespie might have used Mel for . . .

I ought to call Mel, I thought. I ought to tell him. If— he doesn't know.

I got the outside line without any trouble, for a wonder, and dialed the SAE house. A sleepy voice answered, "Mel? Yeah—I'll call him."

"Mel," I said when he came, "you'd better come over here."

"Why? Is Mother—" Alarm came awake in his voice. He must have thought for a moment that she had carried out that suicide threat.

"No. No. It isn't your mother—at least, I don't suppose there's anything wrong with her. I haven't seen her this morning. But—Mel, Mr. Gillespie's dead. He's—he's lying dead out in the garden. Murdered."

"You're putting me on." After a moment he decided I wasn't. "Who— How—" Perfectly normal reactions, I noted to myself, and felt a little better about Mel. I told him all I knew. He said, "Does Mother know?" I supposed not, though I didn't really know. In my naïveté I thought nobody knew but me and Frank and the police. And whoever killed him, of course.

"I'll be right there," Mel said, and the receiver clicked. I'd better go back out to the garden and meet him when he comes, I thought. I washed my face and brushed my hair back and hurried over to the scene-of-the-crime.

How the news got around so quickly I'll never know. But the garden was full of people. Standing around the way they will at any accident, looking horrified and vaguely sympathetic and awfully in the way. A local reporter, Tim Sanders, who was also AP correspondent, was buzzing around asking questions, getting a lot of unofficial and probably irrelevant information. I managed to avoid him myself.

Mr. Bridgewater and a couple of uniformed policemen were holding people back from getting near the body, but if there had been any clues on the surrounding ground they would have been trampled on by now. A man in plain clothes, (who, I found out later, was Lieutenant Dopey Ayres, superintendent of detectives—all three of them) was on one knee beside the body, and I recognized Dr. Mabie kneeling there with him, saying, "He couldn't have made a sound after those hands went around his throat. Pretty strong assailant you've got to look for, lieutenant. A man who could choke him and beat his head on the rock till he was dead—"

I realized in the back of my mind that I had known Dr. Mabie was coroner too, but I had never thought about it before—about what it meant: that he must examine everybody who died in this town without an attending physician to sign a death certificate. Dr. Mabie had taken out my appendix unexpectedly last year—Dr. Fall, the college infirmary doctor, doesn't do surgery.

Lieutenant Ayres was stumblingly reading aloud the Bible verse, holding it carefully by the edges, " 'No man shall take the—the nether or the upper millstone to pledge, for he taketh a man's life to pledge.' Now, Doc, what the hell do you reckon that means? This is a millstone right here."

"It looks like it was cut out of a Bible," Dr. Mabie said. "My pastor could tell you what it means, I guess. It beats me."

The high excited voice of Mrs. Sophie Nelson broke in, seeming to squeeze between the two. "I can tell you what it means," she said. It was the early hour, no doubt; she didn't seem nearly as hazy as she had the day before.

Lieutenant Ayres got up and came over to her, taking a notebook out of his pocket. "What do you know about this affair, ma'am?" he said. "What's your name, please?"

"I don't know a thing about it, officer," Mrs. Nelson said quickly. "I didn't mean I know what it means *being* there. But I know what the Bible verse itself means. I'm using that part of the Bible in my novel, *Moses and Miriam*. It's from Deuteronomy—one of the Laws, you know. It means literally that if a miller should owe someone some money, the creditor may not take his millstone for the debt, since that would be taking away his means of livelihood. Figuratively, it means that no man shall take away another's means of livelihood."

She spoke with surprising dignity; I was proud of old Sophie. And I wondered swiftly, whose livelihood could

Carlton Gillespie have been threatening? That would certainly seem to let Mel's motive, if it was one, out. Unless it was a pure red herring, of course. What about Dory and his painting? But you'd have to stretch a lot of points to call his painting a livelihood, I thought. He hadn't said anything about ever having *sold* a painting. The Bible bit did seem more like Dory than Mel, though. I don't much think Mel ever reads the Bible. Or anything. Our relationship, such as it is, has been purely physical.

Lieutenant Ayres was writing down Mrs. Nelson's name and home address and telling her he wanted to talk with her later. "And all of you," he added sternly. "Don't anybody leave this place—the center, I mean. I'll talk separately to everybody who knew this man, in just a little while."

He went back to the doctor. "Can you give me an idea of how long he's been dead?"

"It'll take an autopsy to prove it," Dr. Mabie said, "but I'd place the time of death at somewhere between eleven-thirty P.M. and one A.M. At"—he squinted at Mr. Gillespie's broken watch face—"approximately twelve-five." He got up and spread with finality over Mr. Gillespie's body the blanket somebody had brought.

"Then *we*'ve got an alibi, Sophie!" I heard Mrs. Annabel Strickland saying excitedly to Mrs. Nelson. She had read murder mysteries too, I thought sardonically. Alibi! What would she need with an alibi? "Remember, we were in the coffee shop then, and I was surprised when I noticed how late it was. We were talking to Mr. Phillips—we practically kidnapped him and made him sit down with us —and it was such an interesting conversation—we talked and talked, didn't we, Mr. Phillips?"

"You did indeed," Mr. Phillips confirmed tiredly, as if he remembered every tedious moment in unforgettable detail; he said "you" instead of "we," I noticed. The way his gaunt head and shoulders were bent from his height, I thought, he looked appropriately like a buzzard at the place of death.

"Well, I've got an alibi too, then." Miss Marianna De-Brett wasn't to be outdone by the other ladies. "And so has Miss Ruskin. Because we were together in her room until after midnight talking about *God's Garden*. It was a Conference. She has lots of Inspirational Writers in her Stable," she added importantly, to nobody in particular. I looked around to see how the literary agent was taking this advertisement, but Miss Ruskin wasn't among this curious crowd.

"*What* garden?" Lieutenant Ayres said.

"It's not a real garden like this one," Miss DeBrett explained to him kindly, patronizingly. "It's a Book I'm writing. Aren't you familiar, Officer, with that Lovely Quotation (I'm using it in the Front of the Book if the Copyright Owner doesn't Object), 'We are Nearer to God in a Garden, than Anywhere Else on Earth'?" Then the aptness of that bit, in the present circumstances—for Mr. Gillespie at least—struck her, and she gasped, "Oh, my Goodness!" and retreated rapidly from the limelight.

"The rest of you people with alibis give 'em to me later," Lieutenant Ayres said sarcastically to the crowd of us. It occurred to me that I didn't have any alibi myself, and I was probably the last person to see Carlton Gillespie alive. Except the murderer, of course.

I saw Mel Alston at last, at the edge of the garden, making his way toward Dr. Mabie. The doctor saw him and spoke to the lieutenant in an undertone, probably telling him who Mel was.

Mel looked down at the shape under the blanket, and his face was unreadable. I guess it's a good thing it was. No telling what would have shown on mine if the dead man had been *my* stepfather whom I hated.

"He's—dead?" he asked unnecessarily.

"Yes. By the way, how did you find out there'd been a death? You weren't staying here at the center, were you, Mr. Alston?" Lieutenant Ayres, I noticed, was a bit brighter than I'd been giving him credit for. I had been thinking that if he weren't a small-town-type policeman he'd have cleared the crowd out of the garden when he first got there. But now I perceived there might be a reason for letting everybody stay; he might think he could learn things from their attitudes and comments.

"Why"—I could see Mel trying to decide whether he needed to protect me by concealing the fact that I had called him, and deciding there was no harm in its being known—"a friend of mine called me. She—she said she was the one who—first saw him."

"And who was this friend?" As if he didn't know. As if Frank Benton hadn't told them when he first called the police.

"Miss Libby Clark. She's attending this writers' conference here at the center."

He looked around for me, and I smiled at him reassuringly. Lieutenant Ayres looked at me, too, and said, "I want to see you in a few minutes."

"All right. I'll be around."

"You'll *all* be around," the lieutenant said sternly.

"You can all go and eat breakfast now if you want to—and dress—" He looked pointedly at Miss DeBrett's perfectly proper plain dark blue robe, and then at Mrs. Nelson's hair curlers, and they both gasped, "Oh, My Goodness!" and scurried down the path toward the center. The words trailed back—"I didn't Realize—" in Miss DeBrett's mortified-to-death voice, with a capital *R*.

A police photographer had arrived in the meantime and had uncovered the body again, and he and the newspaper photographer both started to take pictures from every angle, in a thoroughly emotionless way. Mel turned his back on the scene.

"But," the lieutenant went on, "don't anybody leave these buildings. You can go on holding your convention. But don't go away. I'll call you one at a time, to have you tell me what you know about this."

"We don't know anything about it." It was the first time Van Saylor had spoken. "Why should we? We're holding a writers' conference here, and Mr. Gillespie's death couldn't have anything to do with us."

"Why couldn't it? He was a writer, wasn't he?" Lieutenant Ayres sounded as though he thought of writers as a species of inexplicable fauna about whom almost anything could be said without successful contradiction.

"Maybe he was killed for his money," Mr. Saylor offered with a certain callous note in his voice. "He was probably the wealthiest writer here. Had you thought of that? Possibly some robber surprised him and killed him for his wallet."

Lieutenant Ayres made a note in his book, but I thought it was probably a reminder to check on Mr. Saylor's rea-

63

sons for mentioning it rather than on Mr. Gillespie's wallet. Still, there might be quite something in the suggestion of money as a motive, I let myself muse again. I recalled the man on the phone who had to pay Mr. Gillespie the money he owed him right now, or else—That man, whoever he was, was off the hook now. I tried to think whether or not the voice had sounded anything like Van Saylor's. I couldn't convince myself that it did. Or that it didn't.

The ambulance from the hospital drove up then outside the garden, and an intern hurried in as importantly as if he were the first doctor on the scene. Dr. Mabie just said, "Take him to Harper's."

Harper's is the combined undertaker's and furniture store for this cultural little college town. I felt sympathy for the young intern. He had wanted so much to use his stethoscope in public; he kept fingering it lovingly. Maybe he had even wanted to be the one to pronounce him dead, as they say in the murder novels.

"I've got to go and tell my mother," Mel Alston said. "Unless somebody else has already done it." He looked around inquiringly and got no answer. "Doctor, I wonder if you have time—She may need a doctor when she hears. She might go into shock or something. She was pretty upset last night—"

"Yes, of course. I'll come with you," Dr. Mabie said.

"I will too," Lieutenant Ayres said significantly. "What was she upset about, Mr. Alston?"

They moved away toward the center, and I suppose Mel had to tell them what his mother was upset about. But he didn't know the thing about Kay Hawes, I remembered—unless Mrs. Gillespie had told him. Probably she had,

though. I wondered if the faculty members on the confer-
ence staff had been called—they lived out in town, the
Dean and Dr. Petersen and Larry Mims. And Professor
Hawes.

"Will you have breakfast with me?" Van Saylor was
saying to me, and I didn't believe I could face that prospect—his greenish sports coat on top of the things I had
already gone through that morning.

"I'm not hungry," I said truly.

"Then at least come to the coffee shop and have some
coffee. You look like you need a bracer."

"Thanks, but some other time. I've got to see Mr. Brent
right now."

It was then that I cornered Hamlyn Brent and asked
him about doing my mystery book about *this* murder. He
was walking toward the lobby, not-smoking that omni-
present cigarette in the black holder, and I walked along
with him. After he had given my project his blessing—if
you could call anything so sarcastic a blessing—I asked
him, "Did you know Mr. Gillespie, Mr. Brent? I mean,
before the conference?"

"I've seen him around in New York," he said. "Literary
cocktail parties and things like that. We have the same
agent and know a good many of the same people. But—
we didn't exactly have each other over for dinner."

"He seems to have been a sort of complex character,"
I speculated. "I guess that's the most interesting kind for
a book."

"Not complex," Mr. Brent said. "You could foresee
what he would do in any given circumstance. Just a man
outwardly a gentleman, inwardly a heel, that's all. A very

fine victim for a murder mystery, Miss Clark. The reader mustn't ever like the victim, you know."

"Or the murderer," I said. I was marveling that his snap judgment of Carlton Gillespie should so coincide with mine, when he didn't know all I knew about Kay Hawes and *The Passionate Circumstance*.

"Look, Mr. Brent," I said, "how about an appointment for a talk with you? About my book. Aren't you having individual conferences with writers, like Dr. Petersen and the other workshop staff members?"

"Certainly," he said. "Tonight you write up what you have, so far, and bring it with you to the workshop tomorrow. I'll see you after the workshop. I doubt that we'll have classes today, but I assume the conference *will* go on after the police get through their questioning."

"Thanks. I'll do that."

I thought he was heading for the dining room, but instead he seemed to be going upstairs, too.

Frank Benton was off duty by now, but he wouldn't think of missing any of the excitement. He was still at the desk with the day clerk, talking with a cluster of the guests who stood around surmising. I said, "Frank, is that fool elevator running yet?"

"I'll take you up in it, Libby," he said. "It just wants to be shown who's boss, that's all."

Mr. Brent and I stepped inside, and sure enough, Frank made the old thing start without any trouble. "See?" he said to me, and to Mr. Brent, "Room all right, Mr. Brent?"

"Oh, yes, quite all right," Mr. Brent replied, with that note of irony in his voice that seemed always to accompany his simplest remark.

66

"Nice of you to be so agreeable about it," Frank went on, making conversation.

"Isn't everybody?" I said.

"No. You'd be surprised at the way some of these temperamental writers complain and want to change rooms at the most inconvenient times. You satisfied with yours, Libby?"

"Well, it's not like the one I had at the Paradise-Hilton, but I'll keep it," I said, stepping out when he opened the door at the third floor. "If you'll have it air-conditioned by tomorrow. Thanks for running this diabolical machine for me, Frank."

"Any time," he said.

Mr. Brent stepped out, too, and both the elevator doors, the inner grill and the outer heavy one, slid shut without any trouble. They'd have balked if I'd been the one trying to close them in order to get that elevator to move.

"Well. Your floor, too," I said inanely.

He came with me all the way to my door and then nodded goodbye and went on—to the next door, taking out his key to open it.

"We're—next door to each other!" I said stupidly. Something in my subconscious bothered me about that, but I couldn't quite pin down what it was.

So it was Hamlyn Brent I had barricaded the door against last night. I felt foolish. But I reminded myself that he could hardly have known about that.

Mr. Brent smiled noncommittally (he can even *smile* in an ironical tone of voice), and I went in and shut the door, furious at myself for saying something he might have misinterpreted. What did he *think* I meant?

I was just rolling up my hair when the phone rang.

It was Mr. Bridgewater, sounding anxious. Mr. Bridgewater and I are old friends; I always stop to talk with him when I meet him on the campus, and sometimes we have what he calls a date, when he takes me over to the co-op for a Coke. He's been the campus policeman for a good many years—since before they were called security guards, in fact. But he's too old for any really active police work. It's a way of pensioning him off (since he used to be on the force) while letting him feel he's still working, still useful. And he *is* useful, of course; he knows so much about the college; he's *much* more than a security guard.

He said now, "Libby, Lieutenant Ayres wants to see you."

"All right. Where is he?"

"He's set up shop in a room on the second floor—one of the workshop rooms, two-oh-one. Libby"—he sounded anxious—"somebody told him they saw you going toward the garden last night a bit after eleven-thirty, in a yellow dress. Did you wear a yellow dress last night?"

"Why, yes, Mr. Bridgewater, I went down there. I had a date. In a yellow dress. What's wrong about that?"

"That was awfully close to the time they say Mr. Gillespie was killed down there, child."

"I know," I said. "I saw him, Mr. Bridgewater. But he was alive then. It was when I was leaving. I might have been the last one to see him alive."

"Somebody was with you, then? You had a date?"

"No. My date didn't come. What do you know about that—he stood me up!"

"Anybody with Mr. Gillespie?"

"No. But never mind about an alibi for me, Mr.

68

Bridgewater. I didn't have any reason to kill a man I'd barely met."

He said troubledly, "A girl couldn't have—But I hate for you to get mixed up in such a thing as this, child."

"It's all right, Mr. Bridgewater. I'm going to use it for my mystery story for the conference workshop. All the details will come in handy. You try to remember everything for me. From what I've heard, lots of people thought Mr. Gillespie wasn't exactly fit to live, anyhow."

"You come on down here and see the lieutenant, Libby. And don't let him hear you say things like that. And if I was you, I'd write some other kind of books."

I went, right away. In the corridor on the second floor I met Mel. He was white-faced and disturbed.

"I haven't had a chance yet to thank you for calling me this morning, Libby," he said. "Lord, I wish I'd been able to get with you at eleven-thirty last night. That man seems to think I—I might have—I wish there were somebody besides Mother to say where I was. He seems to think Mother might have wanted me to—He seems to think she's lying about something. He doesn't have any human feeling for her at all. She *cared* about Gil, Libby. That's why what he was doing to her was so bad. She wouldn't have wanted him dead. She might have wished Elaine Westover dead, but not Gil. We didn't know anything about what he was doing last night. Mother told them he said it was a man—well, someone; it could have been a woman, writer or agent—he was going to see, for something about writing. But they nagged her into admitting that when he didn't come in all night she thought he was probably lying—that he was spending the night with that woman somewhere. There had been gossip, and the police

69

listen to gossip and make guesses. Van Saylor, for one, told them some of the rumors. They're still questioning Mother—alone. They made me leave after they took my fingerprints." He looked at his smeared fingertips as if he could hardly believe they were his.

"The lieutenant sent for me," I told him. "It won't hurt, will it, to admit that we had a date last night in the garden but that you had to stay with your mother and didn't come? Somebody saw me going there."

"It won't make any difference," he said wearily. "I told him. They'll find out anything they want to know, anyway. No reason why they shouldn't know. Only I wish I *had* been with you."

"Mel," I said impulsively and with sympathy, putting my hand on his arm, "this is tough on you—"

"Tougher on Mother," he amended, adding callously, "I didn't like him, you know. I won't miss him. Somehow it doesn't seem to touch me at all. But Carla—she was crazy about him. He had her completely snowed. Poor kid —she'll probably go to pieces. I've got to go and phone her now."

"I guess she'll come, won't she?"

"I guess so. I wish she needn't. But of course she will. Probably fly down as soon as she can catch a plane."

"Let me know if I can help at all," I said as people always do in cases like this. As if anybody could help, if Carla loved him.

While Mel said, "Thanks," and went on, his face drawn and worried, I stood there pondering how, no matter what a heel a person may be, there's always somebody who loves him and is blind to his faults and suffers when anything happens to him. Even if it's only a dog. This time it was Carla. Mrs. Gillespie, too, of course, but she wasn't exactly blind to his faults, was she? She just loved him in spite of them, and that was even more pitiful, when you came to think about it.

But I could see how Lieutenant Ayres might suspect her of being fed up and angry enough to kill on impulse. Jealousy was a prime motive. And in that case she would have had to have Mel's help.

The story he told me could have been true, up to a point —and then they could both have gone to the garden and have been in the quince thicket waiting to surprise the lovers at their rendezvous and confront them. . . . That's what Lieutenant Ayres would think, anyhow. I didn't exactly believe it myself, but the possibility was alive enough to make me uncomfortable.

Mrs. Gillespie came out of 201 and went off down the hall toward the elevator, looking dazedly at her smudged fingertips and not seeming to see me, so I thought I wouldn't offer sympathy right then. Dr. Mabie came out of the room after her, looking as if he wanted to be sure she could make it by herself all right, and rather doubting it.

"Dr. Mabie," I said.

"Oh, hello, Libby. I think Ayres must be waiting for you. He said a while ago—"

"I suppose there's going to be an inquest?" I said. "Could I come to it, Dr. Mabie? You see, I'm studying the writing of murder mysteries, and I thought I might write one about this case."

"What do you want to do that for?" he asked irritably. "Why don't you write about something pleasant?"

"This way you meet such interesting policemen," I said,

perhaps too flippantly. "I really ought to know what the inquest is like, Doctor—"

"Oh, you'll have a chance to find out, all right," he said. "You'll be there, giving evidence. You're the one who found the body."

"That's right! I will be there, won't I?" I didn't exactly feel delight at the prospect, but I did feel excitement. I was getting very valuable experience for my writing, no doubt about it. Anybody who complained that writers' conferences didn't help a writer much sure ought to be at this one.

"You go on in there and tell Lieutenant Ayres all you know about it," Dr. Mabie said dryly. "You needn't save anything for the inquest. You can tell it over again."

With reservations I will, I thought. Not about Kay Hawes. But I would tell the strict truth about everything they already knew to ask me about, and I would volunteer the news about the telephone conversation I overheard.

As I thought it would, that phone conversation interested Lieutenant Ayres quite a lot. He had a man taking down every word I said, even the repetitions—and there were a lot of those, because he kept asking and I couldn't possibly tell him whose voice the hoarse and surely disguised voice sounded like. He asked me all about my being in the garden, too. I told him about that feeling I had of being watched, and about seeing Mr. Gillespie arrive, and the words I heard him exclaim: "So it's you! I *thought*—"

"And this was at what time exactly, Miss Clark?"

"It must have been about twenty minutes to twelve. I had been looking at my watch, you see—the moon was bright enough—because I was trying to decide how long to wait for my date. I figured ten minutes was quite long enough. It was twenty to twelve when I started to leave, and right after that when I saw Mr. Gillespie coming."

He had already asked me, while they were fingerprinting me, about whether I had seen the meeting in the coffee shop when Dory Pevlin attacked Mr. Gillespie, and now he went back to that. "Did Pevlin seem to you capable of actually killing Mr. Gillespie, like he threatened?" he asked. I suppose if a detective wasn't around when something significant happened, he had to ask people who *were* there to tell him about it. And see if they all saw the same things.

"He didn't exactly threaten to," I said. "He just said he ought to."

"Well, did he sound like he would do it?"

"Frankly, no," I said. "Dory Pevlin doesn't seem to me the man-of-action type. He's the kind who'll talk big and never do anything about it. He wouldn't have attacked Mr. Gillespie at all if he hadn't been drunk—or high on something. He probably would have avoided him."

"Yes, but he *was* drunk," the lieutenant said. "Do you think he could have killed him on sudden impulse, in a rage, if he *was* drunk?" He was asking me to speculate now on what *could* have happened. Was he just trying to draw me out, to find out more about *me?* But I didn't mind speculating. It was sort of fun, sparring with a detective.

"He looks strong enough to, if that's what you mean," I said. "But the Dean and Mr. Mims put him to bed. At least, I suppose they did—you could ask them. They took him out. I think once he was lying down he'd have stayed there until he slept it off. It would have been too much trouble for him to get up again and go out and kill Mr. Gillespie."

"A lot you know about drunks," Lieutenant Ayres muttered. And I bet he hasn't been to as many fraternity house parties as I have.

"You asked me what I thought," I pointed out. "After all, I've taken Psychology 7, Lieutenant. Writers need a lot of psychology."

"Writers!" He said it as if it were a four-letter word. "And do you have a pen name too, like the rest of them?" he inquired with sarcastic interest.

"Not yet," I said. "But no doubt I will have when I write enough to need one. It's perfectly legitimate for a writer to use as many different names as she needs."

"So I hear," he grunted. "So everybody has an alias—"

"A pen name isn't exactly an alias, Lieutenant," I said gently. "And does everybody except me have an alibi, too?" I asked him, wanting very much to know—for literary purposes. He simply ignored the question.

"That's all for right now, Miss Clark," he said. "You stick around this area, hear?"

"All right, Lieutenant. As a matter of fact," I added daringly, "I'd like to stay right here with you and watch you work, if you don't mind. You see, I'm writing a murder mystery about this murder, and—"

"Are you out of your mind, young lady?" he said simply, motioning to the cop by the door to open it for me. And I realized, as it closed behind me, that the people in the murder novels who are in on all the detective work are allowed there because they know the writer, not the detective. The author can let them stay if she likes, but the police won't.

But I still had Mr. Bridgewater up my sleeve, as Mrs. Strickland would say.

5

Still Tuesday Morning

Well, all right, I said to myself, feeling definitely snubbed. If they won't help me, I'm not going to help them. From now on, I won't tell them a thing I find out. And I'm *glad* I didn't say anything about Kay Hawes and *The Passionate Circumstance*.

I went down to the lobby to look at the bulletin board and see if the conference really was going to go on as if nothing had happened. Yes; Mr. Phillips's talk would be in the auditorium at two P.M.; the workshops would start at 3:30 in the various assembly rooms on the second floor. The poetry one was rerouted from 201 to 217.

Miss Marianna DeBrett was looking at the notice, too. "Do you think they should go right on with this conference as if nothing had happened, Libby?" she said. "It seems somehow Lacking in Respect, doesn't it?"

"And it could be dangerous for the rest of us, too," Van Saylor added, coming up in time to hear her. "Do you realize that there could be a murderer right here among us?"

Miss DeBrett gave a little scream and moved away from him suspiciously. "Don't frighten us like that," she said faintly.

"Let's try not to worry about it," I said hardily. "If Dean Crossett thinks it's O.K. to continue, I'm with him." Of course they couldn't stop the conference now; it would ruin my chances of getting material for my great mystery book.

Ms. Maude Ruskin put in from a nearby sofa, "I'm not afraid of being a victim. After all, if somebody had a reason to kill poor Carlton, there wouldn't be the same reason to kill any of the rest of us." She sounded very calm about losing one of her writers; she couldn't have liked him much herself.

Miss DeBrett bought that. "Why, that's true," she said. "I guess we don't need to be afraid, after all. And the police did say we *have* to stay here, so we might as well be going to workshops, to Take Our Minds Off."

"Besides," I said, "who says the murderer is right here among us?" I scowled at Van Saylor. "He could be a strange bum who wandered into the garden and mugged Mr. Gillespie for his money."

"So he could," Hamlyn Brent agreed softly into my starboard ear. He had strolled up behind me. "But it won't do your plot any good, Miss Clark, to let the murderer be a stranger. It would be better if he turned out to be—say —somebody like me." He smiled like Mephistopheles and sat down beside Ms. Ruskin. It was sort of hard to remember always to call her Ms., but I tried to because Serena Wilcox had said she liked to be addressed that way.

As I turned away from the bulletin board, Mrs. Annabel Strickland summoned me excitedly from a sofa where she and Mrs. Sophie Nelson were sitting. I went over and sat with them for a moment.

"What do you think?" Mrs. Strickland cried. She had on her brown sack now, probably dyed with the same walnut hulls she uses on her hair.

"Have you got a plant that dyes blue?" I asked, fascinated, in spite of everything, by the herbivarous possibilities. "No, I don't think we're all going to be murdered, Mrs. Strickland."

"Yes. Indigo. It's got long sprays of blue-purplish flowers," she answered parenthetically, and then went on with what she had been about to tell me. "They were looking at all the Gideon Bibles in all the rooms—the policemen were—to see which one the verse was cut out of—and Sophie's is missing!"

"They don't think Mrs. Nelson—?" I smiled at Sophie.

"No, of course not. We've got an alibi, remember? We were talking to Mr. Phillips in the coffee shop at twelve-five. But they think maybe the murderer took her Bible to cut the verse out of instead of his own."

"What was he doing in her room?" I asked, almost feeling as though "he" were a real person, not just a hypothetical murderer. I could almost see him, a shadowy male figure, not anything outstanding as a man, of course, not tall or short, not stout or thin. *Not anybody I knew.* Ordinary—and faceless.

"Oh, he could have gotten in, all right. When the maid

left it open while she was cleaning on that floor. Or actually, I bet these keys will open any of the doors. They look like plain old skeleton keys. I've got a good mind to try it and see."

"Let's go try yours on my door right now," I said. "It would be useful to know if somebody can get into a room whenever he wants to. Especially if there's a murderer loose around here."

Frank wasn't around, but Mrs. Nelson showed an unexpected competence in cussing the elevator, in her stately blurred fashion, and we rode up. Clustered around my door, trying the key, we must have looked odd to Mr. Brent as he came out of his room next door.

"Having trouble with your key?" he asked.

"We thought maybe these were just skeleton keys that would open any of the doors," Mrs. Strickland explained eagerly. "So if the murderer wanted to—you see, somebody took Sophie's Bible out of her room—it may be the one the verse was cut out of—"

She was telling him entirely too much, I thought objectively. If you knew any little thing and you told anybody about it, he might turn out to be the murderer and you might be the next victim. If what you knew had any bearing on the murder and he needed to keep it from being discovered, even though you didn't realize it was important at all—

But I didn't see how what Mrs. Strickland suspected could be important. Because in fact her key wouldn't open my door. Nor would Mrs. Nelson's. And mine wouldn't open theirs when we tried later. We had to give up the skeleton-key theory.

Mr. Brent just looked amused and went on downstairs with us. I could tell he thought I was just playing at being a detective, and that particular incident did seem sort of childish. I vowed to myself that I would find out something that *would* prove significant. I had an idea in the back of my head. Of course I didn't really think Professor Hawes would kill anybody, even if driven to it by a desperate reason, but I wanted mightily to know how much of a reason he had. The only way to find out was to get hold of the proofs of that book—if Mr. Gillespie hadn't sent them back before he was killed.

I went to the house phone and called the Gillespies' room, making sure (I thought) that nobody could overhear. As I figured he might, Mel answered.

"Mel," I said, "I know it's none of my business, and *don't* mention it to that detective, but I've got an idea there may be a clue to the murder in that book Mr. Gillespie was correcting the galleys on. How would you and your mother feel about letting me read those galleys?"

"You still writing a story, Libby?" he asked tiredly. "I don't see how the book could have anything to do with it, but the proofs are still here, and if you want to read them I don't see how it could do any harm. When do you want them?"

"I guess tonight would be good enough," I said. "It's nearly lunchtime, and after that we have to go to Mr. Phillips's talk and then to a workshop. Tell you what, I'll get the galleys from you at the barbecue, if you'll bring them, and read them afterwards, during the evening. How's that?"

"Okay."

"Thanks, Mel."

I turned from the phone and almost ran into Professor and Mrs. Hawes. It was the first time I had seen them since yesterday's picnic.

"Oh, did they make you come and be questioned, too?" I said. I wanted to reassure them that I hadn't mentioned the discussion about the novel to the police, but I didn't know how. It would seem far too pointed just to tell them bluntly.

"They've already finished with us," Professor Hawes said, shrugging. "We couldn't tell them anything, except that Kay knew him a long time ago and hadn't seen him for years until yesterday."

"That ought to be good enough," I said lightly. "I never even met him until yesterday, but because I was probably the last one to see him alive except the killer, and I found the body, they had to talk to me, too."

"Is that so?" Professor Hawes said sympathetically.

"It must have been a shock," Mrs. Hawes murmured. Neither of them looked exactly the way they did on other days, but then *nobody* looked quite the same today. Being questioned by the police will make anybody nervous, and being even on the edge of a murder isn't exactly calming. It didn't have to be guilt. I must have looked like somebody else besides the usual Libby Clark, too.

I saw Mr. Bridgewater just then, ambling toward the door, and I wanted to talk to him. "See you later," I told them. "Probably you'll be at Mr. Phillips's talk? I want to catch Mr. Bridgewater—"

"Sure. See you later," the Professor said amiably.

I caught up with Mr. Bridgewater just outside. He was

going home to lunch, he said. It was Mrs. Gussey's day for meat loaf, he mentioned unenthusiastically.

"Sit down here on this bench with me for a minute," I urged with all the charm I could turn on. "I need some advice."

"Oh, in that case," he agreed readily. We sat there in the shade for a minute without speaking. It felt kind of peaceful to be apart from the center with all the people and talk. The sky was just as clear a blue as if there hadn't been an ugly thing like a murder under it last night.

"How are they getting on?" I asked casually. "Are they finding out anything?"

"Not much," Mr. Bridgewater said. "Lots of stuff comes up, but none of it means anything much. They been arguing for the last half hour about whether to take the millstone in for evidence or not. It's awful heavy." He chuckled. "*And* settled deep in the ground. I think myself they could have the inquest all right without *that* murder weapon."

"When will they have the inquest?"

"Oh, tomorrow or next day, probably. Depends if they decide on an autopsy. Guess they ought to have one, by the law. But Doc is sure Gillespie was being choked at the same time he was being killed by the blows on the stone. It would be some little coincidence, wouldn't it, if they found a bullet in him too."

"What else have they been doing?"

I was glad Mr. Bridgewater was such a garrulous old guy and that he was used to talking to me, because I could see he was my only chance to find out what was being done by the police. Lieutenant Ayres might not want to tell me anything, but Mr. Bridgewater just loved to show me how much he knew.

"Oh, they found out everybody's using another name than their own," he said, and chuckled again. "That bothers Dopey. I tell him it's normal for writers. Professor Hawes is just about the only one that writes under his own name. No—that feller with the funny name does too. Guess his own name was odd enough so he didn't have to make one up. Dory Pevlin," he ruminated, chewing it a bit. "But the rest all have different names. I wrote 'em down because they're so funny." He pulled an old envelope out of his pocket and consulted it. "Would you believe Miss Elaine Westover that writes the poetry, she's really Miss Ellen Burpitt? *Burpitt.* Ain't that something? And Mrs. Serena Wilcox is really Irene Wilks. Mr. Cobb Wilmer just turned his around—he's Wilmer Cobb. And when Mrs. Hawes wrote poetry and worked on the newspaper she was Kay Warden. It was her own name, though."

"Does Van Saylor have another name?" I remembered he had said that was his pen name. "And Mr. Brent? What about Mr. Phillips? He has two already."

"Mr. Saylor is really Fitzgerald Mayo," Mr. Bridgewater revealed importantly. "Mr. Phillips's own name is Paul Barlow. And you'll die at this one, Libby. Mr. Hamlyn Brent is really John Smith."

"No!" I said. I really was surprised. It didn't seem possible, to look at him. He looked much more like Hamlyn Brent.

"You'll like Mr. Fleetwood Barr's, too," Mr. Bridgewater went on complacently. "He was born Victor Quinch.

Don't think I ever run across that name before. There's one more—that Mrs. Strickland. She said her pen name is going to be St. John Friar. Said she thinks a *man* had better sign the kind of novel she's writing. What kind is she writing, eh, Libby?"

"I guess she *thinks* it's going to be pretty sexy," I said. "Actually she knows about as much about sex as a five-year-old. She ought to do some research up your alley, Mr. Bridgewater."

Mr. Bridgewater chuckled happily. I do what I can to bolster his little fantasy that he used to be a devil with the girls and that he's just been holding his virility in check since he got to be a respectable senior citizen.

"I wonder about that Bible verse," I mused. "I wonder whose livelihood Mr. Gillespie was interfering with? That's the key to the whole thing. It couldn't be just a red herring—the murderer took too much trouble with it. He'd have had to cut it out beforehand and have it ready —which means he was planning to kill Mr. Gillespie, and it wasn't a sudden impulse of rage at all, like Lieutenant Ayres suggested it might have been if it were Dory Pevlin. Dory was too drunk to have cut out that verse so neatly."

"He could have fixed it before he got drunk." Mr. Bridgewater surmised that, and quite acutely. I agreed that he could have, but I wasn't convinced that he did.

I went rambling on, thinking out loud. "If they should find the Gideon Bible out of Mrs. Nelson's room in somebody else's room—but there'd have to be two there or they wouldn't know it *was* her missing one—unless they could tell by fingerprints?"

"They'll find it after-while," Mr. Bridgewater said.

"You can't hide a thing as big as that. You could flush the paper part bit by bit down the toilet, but the hard covers would stop it up. And that would give it away. Nobody's reported a stopped-up toilet today. I asked."

"What else did Lieutenant Ayres find out by questioning everybody?" I asked boldly.

"Oh, nothing much. He did find out that Dory Pevlin didn't stay put in his room after the Dean put him to bed. Mr. Brent says he went by to see him later on—about twelve-thirty, that was—and his room was unlocked but he wasn't in it. Mr. Brent says he waited a few minutes and then went on to his own room."

"Oh!" I remembered vividly the small events surrounding my insomnia the night before. "Yes. That checks. I had been in about half an hour before I even undressed—before Mel called—and then I talked to him on the phone awhile, before I heard the sounds next door—when Mr. Brent came in. He has the room next to mine."

"But you didn't hear any sounds over there before that?" Mr. Bridgewater said. "Mr. Brent can't find anybody who saw him around twelve o'clock. If you had heard him earlier—"

"No," I said. "I didn't. But surely they don't suspect him. What reason would he have?"

"They're checking up on everybody's past to try to find a reason," Mr. Bridgewater said. "That is, as much as they can. 'Tain't easy. None of these writers have police records, worse luck."

"Where does Dory Pevlin say he was?" I wanted to know. So much for psychology. A lot I knew about drunks, as Lieutenant Ayres had put it.

"Says he doesn't know. Says he was just wandering around, he thinks. But nobody seems to have seen him, either. He has a notion he tried to go downstairs and the elevator wouldn't move, so he went by the stairs—and sat on them, half passed out, for a while. But he can't prove it. He's Dopey's favorite suspect right now, because he frankly admits he wanted to kill Gillespie. He admitted everything the people in the coffee shop described about the fight was true, about what he said about Gillespie's column making fun of him and all. Dopey asked him why he wanted to kill Gillespie, and he said, 'I just didn't like him. Violently.' Dopey said, 'Would you kill a man for a reason like that?' and Pevlin said, kind of daring him to make something out of it, 'I might.' Dopey said, 'Well, did you?' Pevlin said, 'I hope so. No—I'd have remembered a satisfaction like that, no matter how drunk I was.' "

"I think he would, too," I said, giving psychology another chance.

"Well, say, Libby, you said you wanted advice about something." Mr. Bridgewater chewed on a twig and looked at me with his bright blue eyes expectant in his rosy wrinkled face.

"Well," I said slowly, really wanting his advice but not wanting to get Kay Hawes in trouble, "if I told you something in confidence, could you square it with your conscience to not tell it to Lieutenant Ayres?"

"Dopey don't have to know everything I know," Mr. Bridgewater said. "Unless, of course, it turned out to be a matter of undeniable evidence against the actual murderer. Then I'd have to, you understand. But if you mean just some clue you've found, or some suspicion that isn't proved—why, we could bat it around together and keep it to ourselves while we work on it. Okay?"

"It's not even a suspicion," I said, glad to realize this. "And certainly not proved. But—" and I told him about the cryptic—yet not so cryptic, after all—conversation between the Professor and his wife and the Gillespies at the picnic.

"So you see," I concluded, "Mr. Hawes wanted very much to keep that book from being published—if it's what I think."

"But killing Gillespie wouldn't necessarily keep it from being published, would it?" Mr. Bridgewater said.

"No, but it would keep Mr. Gillespie from telling anybody at the college what it was about—and meanwhile Mr. Hawes might be able to persuade the publishers not to bring it out, if the author was dead and he could convince them it's libelous."

"He couldn't say it's libelous, could he, unless he admitted the things in it were about his wife? She wasn't in the book by her own name, was she?"

"I guess not." I sighed with relief. "So he really didn't have a good motive for actually killing Mr. Gillespie. That conversation isn't really important, even if I do keep it from Lieutenant Ayres in order to avoid scandal about Kay Hawes."

"Wait a minute. The fact that a skunk like Gillespie would publish such things about his past relationship with another man's wife—in such a way that people who used to know them would be sure to recognize her even if the general public didn't—might easily make the husband mad enough to kill. And a jury might even call it justifiable homicide. Professor Hawes might be the one, at that. Though young Alston's motive looks just about as good, to me."

"It wasn't exactly a motive for either of them that fits the Bible verse about taking a man's livelihood, though," I reminded him. "Besides, I don't know yet—until I read it—whether what's in the book is any motive at all or not. And neither did the Haweses. Remember, they hadn't even seen the galleys. It was only Mr. Gillespie's attitude about showing them the proofs that made them think the worst. Or maybe she was just upset about his stealing her poem for the title page and the book title. I was almost sure, from the way she looked when she heard it, that that was what had happened, and then I overheard her mention it to Professor Hawes later. But you wouldn't kill a man for that, would you?"

"Could they have read the proofs that evening, before twelve-five?" Mr. Bridgewater asked.

"They said they were going home, when they left the picnic. But we can ask Mel to find out from his mother. There was hardly time, though—it's a full-length novel. Mel's going to bring me the galleys tonight to read. He doesn't know why, though."

"Well, don't tell him. Or anybody. Because, Libby," he warned me, "if you know anything that's dangerous to a murderer and he finds it out—" He drew his finger significantly across his throat.

"I'll be careful," I promised, and I got up then to let him go on to Mrs. Gussey's and have his lunch. "See you after a while. I've got to go get some food in a hurry if I'm going to make Mr. Phillips's lecture on time."

I sat down with Mrs. Strickland and Mrs. Nelson, who were having second desserts just to keep their second cups of coffee company. Miss DeBrett had already finished.

"What's new?" I asked after I gave my quick order. Those two were as good as a public address system. They managed to hear and relay everything that was broadcast and a good deal that wasn't. Come to think of it, "Sophie's Sidelights" may be a pretty good gossip column, after all.

"Well—" Mrs. Nelson looked sheepish as well as her usual self, while Mrs. Strickland told me, "Sophie's found her Bible."

"Was it—" I asked breathlessly, "was it the one?"

"No," Mrs. Nelson said.

"Go on!"

"She had it in her bag all the time," Mrs. Strickland explained while Mrs. Nelson nodded her head solemnly to affirm every word. "She took it to the conference with Dr. Petersen yesterday so as to have it handy for checking anything she needed a reference for—and forgot about having it. Her bag's so crowded"—here Mrs. Nelson gestured helplessly at the figured-silk bag that was as large as a knitting bag—"and the things she carries around are normally sort of—er—weighty—"

"I just as-ash-assumed the solid thing in there was another bottle," Mrs. Nelson added to the explanation. "Pretty funny, don't you think so? Not a bottle at all—a Bobble—*Bible*. Had the bottle too, of course." She made it elaborately clear, even redundantly so, I thought. All her consonants corroborated her last statement.

"And the verse is still in it?"

"Right there in Deuteronomy."

"Pretty funny," I agreed. So as to the Bible verse, that left the police right back where they started.

Well, not exactly, it turned out. As I was finishing gulping my hot roast beef sandwich, Lieutenant Ayres came in the dining room door. I watched him with interest —and then with more than interest. He seemed to be coming to our table.

He was. He came up and sat down without even asking, in Miss DeBrett's vacant place.

"Miss Clark," he said sternly, "you haven't told me all you know about this thing."

Well, of course I hadn't. But there wasn't anything incriminating in what I knew about Kay Hawes, so I chose to assume it wasn't relevant. "I've told you all I *know,*" I said stoutly, with emphasis.

"We haven't connected you with Mr. Gillespie in the past—yet," he said. "But—"

"And you won't, either, so don't waste your time," I said. "Because I never saw him until yesterday. Really, Lieutenant."

"Well, it's an unusual coincidence," he observed with heavy significance, "that you're the last person to have seen him alive, *and* the one to find the body, *and*"—he paused to give emphasis to the next words—"the one whose room has a Gideon Bible with the verse Deuteronomy 24:6 cut out of it."

That was what he said. He said it was my room's Gideon Bible the murderer used to cut the "nether mill-stone" verse from. I felt as though something heavy—say a Gideon Bible—had hit me a blow on the top of the head.

Then I rallied. Of course it must mean something. But

not what he seemed to think. I couldn't possibly guess what it did mean, at this point.

"A mere red herring," I said airily. "I ask you, Lieutenant—you're a reasonable man. Would I leave it there if I had cut anything out of it to place at the scene of a murder?"

6

Tuesday Afternoon

"There are no fingerprints on it," he said accusingly. "Not even yours."

"Well, I didn't touch it, that's why," I said. "I haven't had time to do any light reading while I've been here, Lieutenant. Looks like none of the other guests of room three-twenty-five over the years ever read the Bible either. I wonder how many Gideon Bibles, if they were tested for fingerprints, would show they're never touched from one year's end to the other? If the maid ever dusted them, she'd wipe off the outside accidental ones, that you might leave there while pushing it out of your way. But of course if there aren't any fingerprints in Deuteronomy either, *and* the verse is cut out, then the murderer must have worn gloves, don't you think? I bet it's hard to cut out a tiny piece like that on such thin paper, wearing gloves. Pretty neat job, wasn't it? Of course, it could be done with a razor blade, instead of scissors, and with something hard placed under the single page—"

"You seem to know a lot about how it could be done," the lieutenant remarked.

"Surmise, mere surmise," I said modestly. "It's not really hard to surmise. Anybody could do it."

"Then you can't explain it?" he said. "You don't know anything about it? You didn't see anything that seemed to indicate an intruder had been in your room?"

I was thinking, without wanting to, it might have been while that door into the next room was unlocked. That would mean—it might be Mr. Brent. Or it might prove just the opposite—that anyone who could so definitely be pinned down as one with the best opportunity would never have been foolish enough to do it.

But then—I thought on and on—there was the faint possibility that someone had slipped in from the hall while the maids had the room open for cleaning, and substituted the cut Bible for the whole one. You couldn't rule out even the maids, when you remembered that famous book where the postman was the murderer. So it wasn't necessarily Mr. Brent who cut the Bible at all. Still, that unlocked door did leave him the one with the most opportunity. I decided just to take some pretty obvious notes to that story conference I was having with him, and keep a few things secret.

"Well?" Lieutenant Ayres said impatiently. "Did you?"

"I was just thinking," I said reprovingly. "An awfully

good thing to do before you answer, I always say. No, as far as I can remember, Lieutenant, there wasn't anything out of place. I haven't missed anything. Did you find any fingerprints anywhere else in the room?" Maybe if I slipped a question in suddenly like that, I thought, he might answer it before he noticed. Sure enough, he did. A plus mark for psychology.

"No. Only yours. And the maid's."

"Ah, but you see, we didn't wear gloves. It's too hot." I was mentally promising myself, however, to put a chair against *both* doors when I went to bed tonight. And the window. It struck me suddenly (and why I didn't think of it last night I'll never know) that the window opened out on a small gallery that passed by all the other windows on that side of the center, too. Why, *any*body could have gotten in, by cutting the hooked screen, if the window was open. And because of the hot weather and the nonfunctioning air conditioning, it usually was. Evidently the screen hadn't been cut, or Lieutenant Ayres would have told me. Or—would he?

"Where are you going to be this afternoon, Miss Clark?" He rose and stood waiting for me to answer.

"Just over at the auditorium hearing Mr. Phillips's lecture on Inspiration and Sex," I said. The auditorium was a separate building, across the courtyard, but still considered part of the center. "And then at Mr. Brent's mystery workshop. Why?"

"I'm not sure yet when the inquest is to be held," he said ominously. "I just want to be sure you're available."

"I'll be right there, making notes," I told him. "I wouldn't miss it."

"Writers!" He swore and strode out of the dining room. We hurried; he had nearly made us late for the Phillips talk.

The Well-Known Writers who were conducting the workshops for the conference were having to earn their money, all right. Besides the classes and the individual conferences and criticism, each one had to make a general auditorium talk to the whole group about some of his experiences and give helpful hints to writers in general. These were in addition to the talks by special imported speakers, such as Maude Ruskin's on literary agents, and Carlton Gillespie's on Carlton Gillespie—if he hadn't gotten murdered.

I was sort of surprised by Mr. Phillips's frankness in his talk. I had known he was bitter about the things he wrote, of course, because of the way he had talked about them to me at the picnic. But I hadn't expected him to make a speech about how degrading it was for a writer to write for money the way he himself did. He spoke well, though. I kept thinking about Abraham Lincoln as he stood up there on the stage with his gaunt bearded face and his deep-set eyes. He told us aspiring writers precisely how to go about writing just for the money—all the time making us feel that we'd be pretty low-down if we did. Nobody knew exactly how to take it. I could see Dean Crossett making a mental note not to have Mr. Phillips at the conference next year.

Mr. Phillips talked about Grub Street as if he lived on it. He passionately hated himself, you could tell, for debasing his Art—or whatever he thought he had had once, talent or genius or ability. He passionately wanted young writers not to do what he had done—not, he said, to give in to mediocrity. Not to let personal tragedy touch the side of you that is a writer. Not to let bitterness make you stop trying for greatness.

"For personal reasons I won't go into right now," he said, with his white knuckles the only sign of emotion, "I started drinking hard when I lost my newspaper job. I drank myself right down to the bottom. My wife, poor girl, stuck with me. She took me and our child to a little cabin we had up in the Smoky Mountains, and tried to get me to write the Great American Novel. I might have done it—if there hadn't been a moonshiner close by. I tried to write, but there was hate paralyzing my fingers, and alcohol paralyzing my brain. My wife died because I was too drunk to get her a doctor when she needed one, when we were up there in the mountains without a telephone. It sounds like something George Gissing might have written, doesn't it? But that night when I knew she was gone, I stopped drinking. I realized at last that the drinking wasn't hurting anybody I wanted to hurt. It wasn't hurting anybody but us. It was too late to help her, but I knew it was up to me to take care of our child. I had to straighten up and pay somehow for my wife's death. I had to get hold of myself and take care of our little girl. I couldn't write the Great American Novel. I couldn't even get another job. But I found I could write and sell—the kind of tripe I sell. It's easy to do—if you've got to make money. I'd have had my old job if—" He stopped without finishing the sentence.

"Who's George Gissing?" Mrs. Strickland whispered to me.

"Later," I whispered back. I knew who George Gissing was, for a wonder. But I was fascinated by this man's confession. He seemed to have some compulsion to purge himself by telling his sorrows to the world.

"I hate the writing I'm doing." Mr. Phillips was almost calm now. "But I'll keep on doing it while I have to, like the rest of the slaves who sell their integrity for—for worse reasons than mine. But I've never stopped hating what it was that brought me to this;" he ended simply, leaving a certain amount of confusion to compete with the flurry of uncertain applause. I thought the applause was mostly of relief because he had ended. The Dean, for one, looked vastly relieved.

"What's he blaming—the hand that feedsh him?" Mrs. Nelson said as we stood up and worked our way toward the exit. She was wavering a little on her feet, I noticed, and it was still early afternoon. "What is he, a Communisht? Does he think somebody owes him a living? What'sh wrong with him is, he'sh quit drinking," she said confidently. "All teetotalers are kind of pshycopathic. Fanatics."

I saw Van Saylor among the others going up to the front to speak to Mr. Phillips, and I thought it was decent of him.

"Is Mr. Saylor a Communist too?" Mrs. Strickland said, watching him.

"Only alleged," I said without laughing. "Never say 'Communist' without putting 'alleged' in front of it."

"Mr. Phillips didn't say much about how to put sex into novels," she complained then. "That's what I wanted to know. My novel hasn't got a bit of sex in it so far, and

97

that's what it's *about*. So that it'll be a best seller. I can't very well ask Dr. Petersen personally about how to get her —uh—"

"Into bed," Sophie Nelson said helpfully.

"—with Jefferson," Mrs. Strickland accepted.

"That's not Communism Mr. Phillips was talking about," I said, skipping Jefferson's and Mrs. Strickland's dilemma. "At least I don't think it is. Social consciousness, maybe. I think that's what they call attitudes like that. Or just screwball."

"I think I'll sit down out there in the fresh air for a minute before Dr. Petershen's workshop," Mrs. Nelson said confidentially. "Mr. Phillipsh made me thirsty just talking about stopping drinking. There'sh a bensh in the shade out there behind that little ol' bush. Come on and sit down there and have a drink," she invited. "Got plenty with me to lasht through the workshop." She smiled pleasedly, and her mouth wobbled loosely around the smile.

"No, thanks," I said. "You go ahead. I'm sorry for that poor mixed-up Mr. Phillips too. I'm going to tell him it was a good talk."

"You come have a drink, then, Annabel," Mrs. Nelson imperiously tried to persuade Mrs. Strickland, who still doesn't drink.

"No, thanks," Mrs. Strickland said. "I think I'll just go up to my room for a minute, Sophie, before the workshop. You'd better, too," she warned meaningly, and I realized she just wanted to go to the bathroom. She often did, but she was bashful about it. Of course Sophie would just tell Dr. Petersen, man-to-man, if she felt like it. I felt a bit sorry for Dr. Petersen, having them both—and their problems—in one workshop. If Sophie managed to get there.

I went to speak to Mr. Phillips. "You convinced me," I said. "I'm never going to write for money. If any publishers should ever want to pay me, I'll say, 'Give it to the Red Cross.' And I'm on my way now to sign the pledge, too. No, seriously, Mr. Phillips, it was a good talk for us beginning writers. We *need* ideals—even if we'd rather have money."

We were the last people left in the auditorium now, and he moved with me toward the exit—going, I guessed, to conduct a workshop on religion. Or sex.

"I hope you'll remember it," he said earnestly as we went out into the white sunshine. "I hope they all will. If just one good writer believes it—"

I couldn't help feeling slightly flattered—and then like a balloon with the air suddenly poofing out, as I realized he couldn't possibly know whether I was a good writer or not. He didn't mean me. "I'd better be getting along to Mr. Brent's mystery workshop," I said. "See you at the barbecue. Goodbye now."

As I left him I met Kay Hawes approaching, going back toward the auditorium. I had seen her at the talk; she must have left something inside, I thought idly. She nodded to me and went on toward Mr. Phillips. I glanced back and realized that she must have felt some sympathy for him, even as I did; she was holding out her hand to him and speaking warmly. His face didn't change a bit, though— it didn't soften in a smile. Just old Abe Lincoln done in marble, I thought, going on to the mystery workshop.

Mr. Brent was at his suave best. He gave us his opinion

of what makes a superlative mystery novel, and I'm afraid *The Mystery Book Mystery* isn't going to make the Brent Top Ten. But at least it isn't a locked-room-puzzle or an obscure-poison one, both of which he says are dated and overdone. Then he suggested that we bring up our own mystery book problems for analysis. Miss DeBrett volunteered that she was thinking of brewing some lupine roots for a poison; was it an *Obscure* Poison? Mr. Brent told her (letting her down rather lightly, I thought) that possibly she was thinking of oleander leaves or foxglove; he didn't know about lupine. She had better check it out. Oleander and foxglove had already been used by other mystery writers, though.

I said rashly—and afterward wished I hadn't, "What about that Bible in my room? Somebody either came in my room and—wearing gloves—cut the verse that was on Mr. Gillespie's body out of the Gideon Bible on the dresser, or else somebody came in with the Bible already cut and substituted it for the one in my room, just to confuse things. How and why could that have been done?"

Mr. Brent inquired, "Is this a fictional problem, Miss Clark? Or are you giving us a real instance? Did that really happen? Miss Clark," he said to the others, "is basing her plot on our current unpleasantness in the Founders' Garden."

"Yes, it did," I said, but suddenly I saw that I shouldn't have said anything about it. It wasn't common knowledge.

"Well, now, let's see," Mr. Brent said thoughtfully, with a frown between his brows. "Anybody have a suggestion? No? Obviously the Bible verse must have some significance to both the murderer and the victim. The murderer, if he is to leave it with the body, must have it with him. He must prepare it during the evening or the day, Monday, since that was the first day of the conference. He can't simply cut it out of the Bible in his own room—and that would seem to let you out, Miss Clark, unless you were deviously using reverse psychology—since the police will immediately look for the Bible that's been cut. The murderer will have to substitute the cut Bible for some other. Does he choose the room to place it in at random, or does he have a reason for the choice? What do you think, Miss Clark? What will your murderer—in your book—have for his reason?"

It seemed to me that his eyes challenged mine. Foolishly or not, I answered honestly, "I think he did it because he found the door unlocked. He's an opportunist."

"On the other hand," he said smoothly, "there's a chance to complicate your plot by letting him plant the Bible in the girl's room to get her suspected. What about that?"

"She's not a lady wrestler—" "A girl couldn't have done it—" "How could a girl bash his head in?" The class was protesting, giving me the benefit of their doubt.

"That's right," he agreed with afterthought. "A girl isn't likely to have done this murder. Women as suspects are out from the beginning. Except that they might have influenced men to do the killing for them."

"If you mean Mel Alston," I said, "he couldn't—in my book—have killed his stepfather. Because it would have distressed his mother and sister very much, and Mel just wouldn't. Psychology 7."

"But suppose his mother wanted him to do it—urged

him?" Mr. Brent questioned. "Just for fictional purposes, of course. Be objective about it, now, Miss Clark. He had a good motive, his mother's jealousy. He had the opportunity—no one saw him during the crucial time but his mother. The means were at hand—the necessary brute strength and the millstone to batter the head against. Wouldn't he be an excellent suspect?"

"How did you know all that?" I said. "How did you know Mrs. Gillespie was jealous? Do the police let *you* sit in? They wouldn't let me—"

Now it had become a dialogue. The class sat breathlessly listening, not joining in with any speculations.

"No. But I have eyes and ears, Miss Clark. This place is literally buzzing with who did what when. Besides, Mrs. Nelson is in three twenty-eight, across the hall from my room, and I hear her frequently when I go in and out. She discusses *every*thing with somebody. Or even with herself —a regular monologue, I suspect. She has penetration, too, at times. *She* thinks Alston is a good suspect."

"That's true," Marianna DeBrett said. "She told me—"

I had heard Sophie myself, of course. And yes, there were plenty of rumors mixed with facts, with everybody guessing. A murder wasn't something people kept quiet about. Not the unguilty ones, anyway.

"But you've forgotten the Bible verse," I said. "That doesn't fit Mel at all. Sophie herself told us what it means, and she wasn't drinking then. The murder was obviously done by someone whose livelihood was being threatened by Mr. Gillespie. Like the man on the phone."

I had slipped up again. I forgot that I ought not let it out that I knew these things—things that not everybody knew. I saw by Mr. Brent's gleam of real interest that he hadn't heard about *this* through Sophie's wall.

"A telephone conversation?" he asked. "What was it? When?"

"Oh," I said lamely, not knowing how to wiggle out of telling him now, "somebody overheard—the wires must have been crossed—Mr. Gillespie telling somebody to get him the money or else. Money the other guy seemed to have borrowed. And he said something about having to work for him, as the price of blackmail not to tell about the debt, or something. Mr. Gillespie knew the other man couldn't get the money. He was just turning the screws tighter, about doing the work for him, whatever it was. Murder, maybe. Only it backfired—" I was guessing wildly now.

"Is this a known fact or just speculation, Miss Clark? Is it part of your fiction? Do they know who the other man was?" he added, just as eagerly as if he hadn't said that about fiction.

"Mostly speculation, I guess," I admitted. "And no, they don't know who the man was. But they're trying—" I stopped. It had suddenly occurred to me that some idle girl on the switchboard might have been listening in and might have remembered the call and to whom it was made if Mr. Gillespie initiated it. Because it was kind of interesting. But she might not have connected it with the murder, unless she was jogged. And she wouldn't admit she was listening in, unless . . . unless I could find out who was on at that time *and* she happened to be a friend of mine. They have several co-eds working as part-time operators, and Nan Gorman is one of them. She's one of my best friends;

she spent weekend-before-last with me at home, and with rising excitement I thought I remembered that she had mentioned Monday as one of her days to work. Yes, Frank could tell me if she had been on the switchboard at that crucial time.

Mr. Brent had gone back to motive. "You're reading a lot into that Bible verse," he said with that ironic note in his voice again.

"It's a good clue," I maintained stubbornly. "It's the only one with any imagination. It shows one of the writers did it, all right. Not a football player."

"Or a Mugger," Miss DeBrett contributed.

"There's a theory in the profession that after you eliminate all the possible answers to your puzzle, the real solution has to be what's left—even the impossible, Miss Clark," Mr. Brent went on, and I thought absurdly, he's trying to lead me down the garden path—and then I almost laughed at my own mental play on words. "That might mean you should consider having one of the women the killer. Though it seems like a crime no woman could have committed, can you think of *any* way a woman could have done it?"

"No, but I'll give it some thought," I told him. "It would be a great twist for the book if I *could* think of some way."

"Can't anybody help Miss Clark with a suggestion?" Mr. Brent appealed to the class. "Well, suppose we think that one over for our problem for tomorrow. Everybody come in with a solution at tomorrow's workshop. And everybody please bring another problem, from your own plot." Class was dismissed.

I stayed behind for my private conference. But I was uncertain what to confer about. I felt a little wary of Mr. Brent and not at all sure I was skillful enough to match wits with him if he had been the one who had slipped into my room and put that sinister Bible on my dresser. Because if he had been—then the impossible might be true, after all—somehow, he might have killed Mr. Gillespie. But surely he wouldn't do anything to me in a classroom in broad daylight, with people in the corridors outside and the door open.

Then I drew a deep breath and assured myself that I was just imagining things. A man like Mr. Brent couldn't possibly be a murderer. Somebody else had probably gotten into my room. From the gallery? The screen was still hooked on the inside, and not cut or forced open. It wasn't from the gallery. Then when the maid had the room open? I must ask the maid on that floor—though the police had probably already thought of that. Ask her if she left the room open while she went to get something. Oh, there were so many things I needed to know—an amateur like me, not really doing a good detecting job, just getting details for a story. I began to realize what a terrific task the police have, and to feel a little more sympathy for Lieutenant Ayres.

"Well, how are you getting along with your outline?" Mr. Brent said.

"I haven't done much on the actual writing," I admitted. "Things have been happening so fast I haven't had time. But it's going to shape up into a real puzzler, I think. There are so many possible suspects."

"More than two?" he asked. "Not counting the one on

the phone? Dory Pevlin and Mel Alston and who else? As I said, the women would be the best suspects, in fiction. Mrs. Gillespie or Miss Westover—or perhaps Mrs. Hawes?"

"Why Mrs. Hawes?" I said cautiously.

"No reason. Except I heard somebody say Mrs. Gillespie said Kay Warden had known her husband a long time ago when they worked on the *Star-Banner* together. Could there have been something in the past that would make Kay Warden Hawes want to kill Carlton Gillespie? Or have her husband do it for her?"

It was too close. Somebody was surely going to find out. Since there was gossip, the police would surely question Kay and Professor Hawes again, and if she was innocent of the murder itself, she might even tell them the whole story, counting on their keeping it confidential. And they might not believe her. That she was innocent, I mean. I asked myself how I knew she—or Professor Hawes—hadn't done it, and I realized I had no answer except that I liked them, and that people I liked couldn't be murderers.

"Well, help me think up something," I asked him recklessly. "It doesn't have to be true. The less like the actual situation the better, of course. For a novel, naturally, I know the truth has to be disguised. I'm writing it with the real names at first, but later I'm going through it and change all the names and anything that could be identified if it should ever be published. All I want from this real murder is a skeleton plot and the details and atmosphere I can absorb by being right here on the scene. Why, I could never have made up a character like Lieutenant Ayres—"

"Well," Mr. Brent suggested, "suppose they were once

in love, Gillespie and Mrs. Hawes. Suppose he threw her over in some unforgivable way? He *was* a heel, you know, in more ways than one."

"How do you know?" I asked. I suspected it, and so had Dory Pevlin been convinced, but I hadn't known so many other people thought so too.

"Rumors get around," he said, shrugging. "I met him quite a while ago, you know, in New York. There were people, even there, who didn't like him much."

"Well, even if he might have done her wrong years ago," I went along with his supposition just so far, "still —why should she suddenly, after all this time, decide to kill him for it? Or have her husband do it?" I knew a good reason, of course, but I hoped Mr. Brent—and the police —didn't.

"Oh, you can think of something." He shrugged it off now as not his problem and gathered up his books and papers. "We'll talk about it again tomorrow if you like. Maybe you'll have heard some more helpful rumors by then. In the meantime let your subconscious work on it overnight," he advised, and we parted in the corridor.

I will, I promised myself. And also my conscious. While I'm reading *The Passionate Circumstance* in galleys tonight. If it's really so incriminating, maybe I could ask Mel to get his mother to suppress it. She's a decent person, I feel sure. But could they afford the loss of the money? Mr. Gillespie must have gotten a good advance from the publisher. Could they pay it back? And Mr. Gillespie had thought it would surely be a best seller. Would his agent —and Mrs. Gillespie—be generous enough for that sort of expensive gesture?

She might—always supposing she isn't the murderer.

7

Tuesday Evening

The barbecue was held in an open field surrounded by pine trees, below the center and beyond the Founders' Garden. There was plenty of room for an old-fashioned barbecue pit to be dug and for the long tables to be set up.

Dean Crossett went doggedly on with his program for the conference, brushing off reporters like flies and trying bravely to ignore the appalling fact that one of his chief speakers had been murdered. Death comes to all, soon or late, his attitude said, and everything couldn't come to a stop. All those writers would have been disappointed—and he would have had to refund their fees. He did plan to suspend conference activities for a brief memorial service in the chapel at the same time as the funeral in Birmingham, though, he had announced—although as yet nobody knew when the funeral would be. And he had invited another speaker for the Awards Dinner—but he was keeping the name for a surprise.

So all day Tuesday the smoke and smell of the barbecue had floated around the atmosphere, inevitably reminding me of the funeral baked meats in *Hamlet*. John and Charlie, the two porters at the center who claimed to know more about barbecuing meat and making Brunswick stew than anybody else in Alabama, had been constantly busy basting and turning the beef and pork on the spits, slowly, slowly—an all-day job if it was to taste like real Southern-political barbecue and not like something off a roadside stand. Carlton Gillespie lay there in the mortician's slumber room, never to taste barbecue again; Mrs. Gillespie stayed sedated; and the conference went calmly on without them. Well, fairly calmly. Elaine Westover acted just as though she'd never heard of C. G.

As he'd said he would, Mel brought the galleys he had promised to let me read, when he came to the barbecue. I had already gotten my plate of roast meat and Brunswick stew and pickles and rolls and a glass of Russian tea. (Yes, Russian tea again, though I understand Mrs. Petersen had suggested lemonade for a change and had been overruled by Mrs. Crossett, a passionate Russian tea aficionado). The beer alternative was voted down without even being brought up in committee.

But I put my plate and glass down on a pine stump when I saw that Mel had wrapped the proofs in a copy of this afternoon's *Birmingham Star-Banner*. It was only the first edition, of course—the *Star-Banner* takes several hours to be delivered here by truck. But it had the murder on the front page—and a black box around Gil's last column. There was also a subhead: "Campus Beauty Finds Body," and a picture of me that categorically denied the appellation—an awful photo they must have had in the files ever since I won a spelling contest in junior high school. They could have taken a new one if they'd bothered to hunt me up, I thought ruefully. But that's being vain, I reproved myself. In a tragedy like this I shouldn't care what my newspaper picture looks like. It was some comfort to see that Elaine Westover's and even Carla Gillespie's weren't much better. Oh, yes, they had run all the old photos they had in the files, in order to get them in faster in the early editions than they could make new ones. And they had used a picture of everybody who had even the remotest connection with the case. The one they had of Kay Warden Hawes from way back there when she was young, though, was far prettier than mine.

The paper didn't have any new news about the murder, of course, but then there wasn't anything definite enough to print yet. I refolded the paper around the galleys and said, "How's your mother?"

"All right, I guess. Carla'll be here as soon as she can make it. I guess they'll decide about the funeral then. After the inquest. Mother gave them permission to do an autopsy—not that they needed her permission—but Dr. Mabie called a while ago and said the findings weren't any different. He died from the blows on the millstone, but he would have been strangled to death if he hadn't. And the time of death was right. In case you need to know for your story," Mel said without any enthusiasm. "What do you want to read those stupid proofs for?" he asked then. "You said they might have a clue to the murder. What kind of clue? Mother didn't exactly mind your reading them, when I insisted you're—well, somebody special— but she said don't let anybody else see them; it might make trouble for somebody. She's being mysterious about it too."

"I'm not trying to be mysterious," I told him, "but until I see what's in the proofs that might be significant, I don't want to tell you—because it might not be there at all. See? There are plenty of rumors around here already without my starting any new ones. So wait till after I read the proofs, and then I'll tell you all about it."

"Well, okay." Mel wasn't much interested in whether his stepfather's murderer was discovered or not, I could tell. He would probably feel like pinning a medal on him if he was, I thought. And he couldn't have done it himself, or he'd never have brought me the proofs that I said had a clue in them. Unless—he had read the proofs and knew that clue pointed in another direction? That would turn suspicion away from him?

"By the way," I asked, "has Professor Hawes seen these galleys? Or Mrs. Hawes?"

"No," he said. "Nobody's seen them except at a distance. Gil waved them around a lot, but he was secretive about letting them be read."

"That's good." Mel doesn't have much intellectual curiosity; few football players do. He didn't even say, "Why?" He went and got himself a plate of barbecue, and we sat down on a pine log and ate companionably. I do like Mel. He's such a nice normal guy. Restful. *Unless* he's a murderer and a very good actor. But I don't believe that, and I don't see how anybody else seriously could, either.

I was impatient to start reading *The Passionate Circumstance,* so as soon as we finished eating I was ready to go, without standing around socializing. As we were leaving, we met Professor Hawes wandering around irresolutely.

"Hi, Professor," I said. "Where's Mrs. Hawes? Isn't she coming to this elegant affair and get all greasy too?"

"That's just what I was wondering," he said. "She was to meet me here, and I haven't seen her. I thought she might have decided to pass it up and go home instead, but the baby-sitter says no. Kay hasn't been home."

He looked very worried, and with my imagination it wasn't hard to project why. He was afraid she hadn't been able to face the prospect of having her past exposed and had either run away or possibly killed herself in a frenzy of apprehension. Of course she hasn't, I'm sure, but I was guessing that was what was tormenting him, the horrid doubt. People *do* do things like that, the papers say, impossible as it seems when you look at it dispassionately. They get all worked up and upset and they do crazy things. (Psychology 7 again.) But I couldn't think of anything to say that would calm him.

"Well, she's probably just been delayed," I said. "She'll be here soon. Good night, Professor."

"Good night."

I let Mel go upstairs ahead of me while I stopped to ask Frank Benton, who was at the desk again, to check and see which maid had done my room yesterday.

"Doing a little detecting?" he asked cheerfully while he rang the housekeeper's office.

"You know perfectly well I'm writing a mystery book," I said. "Any detecting I do is strictly literary. For the book, not for the police."

He talked to the housekeeper and relayed to me that the

maid I wanted was Cassie, who happened to be on the third floor right now. So I could probably see her as I went to my room.

"Thanks," I said. "Another thing, Frank—who was on the switchboard right after supper last night?"

"That was Nan Gorman. But she won't be on again until tomorrow afternoon."

"I thought it might be Nan," I said with satisfaction. "Well, remind me I want to ask her something."

"Don't tell me Nan done it!"

I was getting pretty tired of Frank's cuteness, but he was useful sometimes. I just said, "Come on and run me up in that foul elevator," and he did. The desk was never very busy.

"There's Cassie now," he said as he closed the elevator door behind me with a minimum of trouble.

The maid was at the door of a linen closet where she had been sorting sheets. I went to speak to her.

"Cassie, did you do the rooms on this floor yesterday?"

"Yes, ma'am, I did."

"Well, do you remember if you happened to leave Room three-twenty-five unlocked while you went to get more towels or soap or anything?"

"No, ma'am. I never leave rooms unlocked. You missing anything?" she asked anxiously. She knew who would be blamed in case something had been stolen. She wouldn't be likely to admit it even if she had left the door open for a moment.

"No, I haven't missed anything and I don't *mind* if you left the door open. I just want to know if anybody could have gotten in there before I came, maybe, or while I was downstairs in the lobby. What time did you do three-twenty-five?"

"Oh, it was real early, about nine-thirty yesterday morning. But all the linen wasn't back then. So last night I went around putting towels in all the rooms. Might've been—" she admitted slowly, "I could've left the door open just a minute while I went back for some more. But it couldn't have been long enough—"

"Nothing was stolen," I assured her again. "What time would that have been, Cassie?"

" 'Round—well, maybe a little before nine."

"Did you see anybody—maybe somebody who isn't on this floor—hanging around then?"

"No, ma'am. The gentleman in three-twenty-seven came up in the elevator and went in his room right after I finished in yours, but he's the only one I seen at all."

"And I came up sometime after nine and left again around ten."

"Yes, ma'am," she said obligingly. I gave her a tip and went on into my room with the galleys. I hadn't gotten very far cross-examining Cassie, I told myself ruefully. I hadn't proved anything except that someone else besides Mr. Brent *might* have swapped the Bibles, and I thought I already knew that. But the gentleman in three-twenty-seven had been on the scene at an opportune time if he had wanted to do it then, right after Cassie had finished in my room.

I've got to get organized, I told myself. I've got to decide what I'm trying to find out, actually. And who's my prime suspect. I've got to either clear them definitely in my own mind, one at a time, or pin it on them some way.

114

I guess detectives really do have to be clever; clearing and pinning aren't easy.

Meantime, my next job was to read *The Passionate Circumstance*. Maybe that would clear Kay Warden Hawes and her husband. At least to me.

I checked the door locks and window-screen latch and sat down at the desk with the proofs. There was no Gideon Bible to get in the way—the police had taken it as Exhibit A or something. I began to read.

I read steadily and with a kind of horrible fascination. With the foreknowledge I had, it was easy to see Kay in the young girl reporter. Mr. Gillespie had a certain facile talent; he brought his characters alive. I was afraid he had brought the young Kay too vividly back to life. After all, it was only ten or eleven years ago. Surely nobody who had known them then—and gossiped about the hot affair of Gil, who was married, and the young girl reporter, who gave him her love with such gallant recklessness—could fail to recognize the character. He had even named her Katharine. As I read it I loathed the hero, Charles Gabriel, with an almost personal loathing. C. G., even.

I had just come to the part where the girl told him she was sure about the baby and that she would not murder it with an abortion, as he suggested, when the knock came at my door. I glanced at my watch; it was after ten. I went to the door.

"Who is it?" I asked cautiously. Mama hadn't brainwashed me for nothing.

"It's Leslie Hawes, Miss Clark."

I opened the door. My subconscious didn't think he would hurt me, even if he might as a far-off possibility have killed Carlton Gillespie. Justifiable homicide, I agreed silently with Mr. Bridgewater.

"May I come in?"

"Of course. Why, Mr. Hawes, what's the matter? Sit down. You look terrible," I said with truth. His eyes were dazed and glassy, seeing something he didn't want to see. He was obviously dreading something very much. His face was pale and tense. He took out his handkerchief and mechanically wiped the sweat from his face.

Then he saw the galleys on the desk and took a step forward, stumbled into the desk chair, grasped them with both hands.

"These!" he said. "*These* are what I came for, Miss Clark!" The words by themselves were almost threatening, I realized with new horror. Was he going to try to kill everybody who knew about what was in the book? He did sound desperate.

"Wait a minute, Professor," I said. "How did you know I had the galleys?"

"I heard you tell him on the phone—" and I realized he had been there just behind me when I was talking to Mel; I had seen him as I turned from the phone. "Well?" he asked harshly. "Did you read them? Did you see what that bastard was trying to do to her?"

"I was reading when you came," I said noncommittally.

"You wouldn't talk about it, would you?" Again I thought of a threat, though the words were almost pleading. "I promised her I'd get these galleys and destroy them. But she must have thought it wasn't possible. She's gone off, Miss Clark—God knows where she is now. She couldn't stand having everybody know. She thought it would hurt my position—and would hurt the children. I

might have persuaded Mrs. Gillespie not to publish it—
I think we could have kept it from coming out. But Kay
was so scared—so pitifully scared—and angry and hurt—"
His voice broke. "She must have gone out of her mind
with worry—she wouldn't have left the children. But she
seemed all right basically—she was scared, but she had it
under control, I thought. I mean she seemed normal
enough—not like somebody who was about to—"

"Look, why do you assume she's run away?" I asked,
ignoring the other possibility that I could tell was on his
mind. "She might be with some of her friends. When was
the last time you saw her?"

"At the Phillips talk in the auditorium. Afterwards she
was planning to go alone—she wouldn't let me go with her
—to see Mrs. Gillespie and ask her not to publish the
book. I thought it was very brave of Kay. Mrs. Gillespie
could have thought of herself as a wronged woman at the
time it all happened, and Kay said honestly that she was,
of course. But Kay was very young then and deceived by
Gillespie. She was wronged, too. I didn't feel it was her
fault. I loved her," he said simply, "from the first moment
I saw her. In spite of what had happened, I loved her then
—and I've loved her ever since. I love her very much."

Somehow now it didn't seem as strange for him to be
in my room telling me all this as it had at first.

"And did she see Mrs. Gillespie?"

"I don't know," he said, blinking, as if the thought
hadn't occurred to him before. "When I left her she was
going back to the auditorium to look for her pen. She had
lost it somewhere and she thought she might have dropped
it in there—at the talk, you know."

"That was when I saw her, I guess," I said. "She spoke

to me and to Mr. Phillips. We had just come out of the auditorium together. But why haven't you asked Mrs. Gillespie if she saw her?"

"I don't know. I've been sort of—frantic—since I began thinking she might have—well, I guess I just couldn't think clearly."

"I'll ask Mel right now to ask his mother." I picked up the phone.

Mel answered. "Mel, Professor Hawes is worried because Mrs. Hawes hasn't come home yet," I explained. "She told him she was going up to see your mother this afternoon. Would you please find out from her if Mrs. Hawes saw her?"

"Sure thing. I was here most of the afternoon myself, but I'll ask her. She just woke up." He came back and reported, "No, Libby. She hasn't seen Mrs. Hawes. Anything I can do?"

"Thanks, no, I guess not. Sorry the phone woke your mother. See you." And I hung up before he could ask any more questions.

"She never went to see Mrs. Gillespie, after all," I told Professor Hawes, trying to sound cheerful and relaxed. "But she probably got to talking to some friend and went home with her or something." I repeated comfortingly.

"No. She wouldn't have done that. She'd have telephoned home. Unless she meant to disappear and thought it would be easier for me not to know anything if the police asked me. They'll be sure to think she ran away because she killed Gillespie. Of course she didn't—she couldn't have—no woman could. Why, she was talking to me about that Bible verse—she thought she knew what it meant in connection with the murder, though she didn't tell me that. But you see she wouldn't be the one since she was speculating about it.

"But if the police ever see this—this so-called novel—they'll think she had a motive and it'll all come out. Oh, poor Kay—she didn't have much money with her—where could she have gone?" He was rapidly going to pieces. I could see him thinking that it wouldn't take any money at all to drop into the river down at Falling Point where it's deepest.

"Please don't worry so. It's been only a few hours." It was inadequate, but it was all I could think of to say.

"So you see, I've got to destroy these." He clutched the galleys in both hands. "Then if she should call, I could tell her I've done what I promised—"

"I understand how you feel, truly I do, Mr. Hawes," I said. "But don't you see how useless it would be to do that? They've got extra galleys at the publishers', and they can run all the proofs they want without any trouble—you know that. You aren't thinking straight. Sure, it would keep anybody—the police, maybe—from reading it right now. But it would be better just to ask Mrs. Gillespie and Mel not to let the book come out. Tell them why. They're decent people; they'll probably agree."

"I can't. Kay was braver than I am. I'm a coward. I can't do it." More psychological certainty, I thought, that he didn't kill Mr. Gillespie.

"You have to. For her," I urged.

"I guess so," he said tiredly.

"Look, I'll call Mel and tell him to come here now," I offered. "Then we can explain it to him. He'll get his mother to agree. She loved Mr. Gillespie, I'm sure, but I'll bet she wasn't deceived into thinking he was any admirable character."

"All right. Call him, please."

Mel came, of course. He made a real effort to take in what I was explaining about the book, but it was an effort. "You mean Gil was writing about Mrs. Hawes?" he said, blinking. "Then, Libby, what you meant about a clue was—was—Say, Professor, did you kill him?" he asked admiringly. "The jury'd probably acquit you—" No, Mel just couldn't have done it himself.

"No, Mr. Alston, I didn't kill him," Professor Hawes said, and I believed him. "And neither did Mrs. Hawes, though we both had probably as good a reason to hate him as the person who did kill him. But if the stuff in that book gets around, the police will think it's a motive for murder. Besides, it would kill my wife," he said grievedly. "Won't you please, for Christ's sake, destroy those galleys and stop the book? I'll pay you—tell your mother I'll give her all the advance and royalties on my next book, which is sure to sell well, they tell me, so it might pay her as much—"

"Hell, Professor, you don't have to do that," Mel said. "I know Mother won't object to not publishing the thing, under those circumstances. Here, you just take these proofs and burn them yourself. We'll tell the publisher it's all off. And they'll want to cancel it if there's any idea that it's libelous. I'll tell Maude Ruskin tomorrow. She can handle it—she was his agent. I knew Gil was pretty rotten, but I thought he was only that way to me. And Mother."

"Thank you, Mr. Alston. Thank you," Professor Hawes said slowly. "My wife will be—very grateful. If you should ever—if I can ever—if you need any coaching in history or—or anything at all—" It was such a pitiful, human, abjectly grateful offer of return for such a favor that it almost made me cry.

"If I could only let her know it's all right—that nobody will know—" He went on. "Maybe she'd come back—"

"She's gone away?" Mel said. "That's tough, Professor. She should have known we wouldn't—"

"But *he* would have," Professor Hawes said. "He was going to publish it. Deliberately. He didn't have any heart at all. And somebody—somebody he did something just as mean to—somebody with more guts than I have—killed him for it. And I'm not sorry. Most of the time I'm sorry even to see a dog that was killed by a car. But I'm not sorry about Carlton Gillespie."

"You know, I'm not doing much crying myself," Mel said.

They left together, the Professor muttering, "I've got to find her," and Mel saying, "She may be at home by now" over and over, like an answer. Which it wasn't. There was no comfort for the Professor, I knew. The poor guy wouldn't sleep that night unless she came home. I vehemently hoped she would.

Then I sat down at the typewriter to start *The Mystery Book Mystery*. At this point I have everything down that has happened up to now. It's beginning to shape up, but I can't exactly see what the shape is going to be.

The inquest is tomorrow. Today, I mean—it's almost morning. I'm going to bed now. With chairs against both doors and some glasses and stuff on the windowsill where they'll be knocked off and wake me if anybody tries to get in.

8

*Wednesday Morning
and Afternoon*

A lot of things happened today, and if I can get them all
down on paper tonight, it may keep them from running
around in such turmoil in my mind, and maybe let me
sleep. Telling something is supposed to release you from
it.

The inquest was a disappointment. I suppose the police
must have some good reason for making it so short and
to the point, but it didn't help *The Mystery Book Mystery*
a bit. They merely identified Carlton Gillespie, established
how dead he is, how and when he died, how and when I
found him, that nobody can be considered a suspect so far,
and concluded that he came to his death at the hands of
a person or persons unknown. Mr. Bridgewater says if
they get a suspect they have any real evidence against,
they'll indict him later. I thought Dr. Mabie might have

dramatized my first inquest a little bit, just to help out my book, but it was all over in time for me to get back to the Center for Maude Ruskin's 10:30 A. M. talk on literary agents.

There were several young reporters from the Birmingham papers at the inquest, as well as the AP and UP men, and they got a better picture of me, I hope, than the one in yesterday's paper. Nobody told me not to talk to them. I figure the publicity may help the sale of my book if it ever gets published. There's some national interest in Carlton Gillespie's murder, since he was already a sort of "well-known author."

Lieutenant Ayres refused to tell the reporters anything; he wouldn't even say he has any suspects, much less admit who they are. "It happened only yesterday," he told them plaintively. "We've only been on it twenty-four hours. Give us a chance, will you? Maybe there'll be something new developing to tell you by tomorrow."

Well, something new developed, all right.

Another murder.

But wait till I come to it.

I saw Mr. Bridgewater just before I went to the auditorium, and he said that, sure enough, Dopey Ayres had the idea that Kay Hawes had disappeared because she had something to do with the murder of Mr. Gillespie. They didn't know how she could have killed him or her motive as yet, but they couldn't see why she would run away if she wasn't guilty. Still, they haven't given up their tentative classification of Dory Pevlin and Mel Alston as suspects either, Mr. Bridgewater reported.

I told him what the maid said—that somebody could

have entered my room with the Bible while she had the door open. He said it was well to know that, but it didn't help much. He also told me something I hadn't realized before: that detectives were unobtrusively stationed here at the center "working on the evidence"—whatever that means—and watching everybody, just in case.

"I'm going down to headquarters now," he said. "Dopey says they've just gotten in some stuff from New York on some of these people's backgrounds. I'd like to know what it is, just out of curiosity. Dawson down there will tell me—we're old buddies. Seems to me people named Quinch and John Smith and such ought to have something kind of interesting in their past."

"Let me know," I said, giving him my best flattering smile, and I went on to phone Professor Hawes before Maude Ruskin's talk. He said no, he hadn't heard from his wife, and I could tell from his voice that he was just about ready for a padded cell. I could hear child noises in the background. I thought, if I didn't have so much else to do I'd go out there and help him. (I had a long career of baby-sitting between twelve and sixteen.) But right now I had to get over to the auditorium.

"Take it easy, Mr. Hawes," I said. "I'm on your side. Not that it'll help any, but—"

"Thank you, Miss Clark," he said sadly. "Indeed you did help last night."

At the auditorium I sat down in the back row with Mrs. Strickland and Mrs. Nelson, who said they had been waiting for hours. Mrs. Nelson was treating her hangover with her usual remedy. "What's new?" I asked them.

"I *know* Mrs. Hawes didn't do it," Mrs. Strickland said.

So the news of her disappearance had been well spread around.

"How do you know?" I was beginning to feel a positive affection for Mrs. Strickland. Vague as she was about ordinary things like time and place, and dressed as she was in her home-dyed outfit (it was the indigo today), she had a way of picking up odd scraps of information, the way birds pick up bright bits of cord or yarn. I wasn't exactly building a nest with them, but I was building *some*thing. I could use them.

"Well, it was this way. I was in the telephone booth yesterday before lunch in that dim little nook off the side of the lobby—you know?—calling my married daughter to see how the children are—they had the chicken pox when I left—and I had the door cracked open because it was so hot in there, so the light wasn't on in the booth. After I hung up I sat there for a minute because I had a sudden idea for my book and I was scribbling it down— Dr. Petersen says to write down every idea that occurs to you in the course of work on a novel, before it gets away from you, and this was a good one about—well, anyhow, I was sitting there half hidden in the dark when Professor and Mrs. Hawes came by outside. I heard her say to him, 'You *didn't* do it, did you, Leslie?' and he said, 'Kay! Of course not! You know I'm the kind of coward that can't even kill a mouse without feeling guilty about taking its life,' and she said, 'Of course I *knew* you didn't—but I thought you might have thought—on account of me—you had to do something—' And then they moved on. But you see," she concluded triumphantly, "if she thought he might have done it, then *she* couldn't have!"

125

"You're right," I said. "That certainly clinches it. You'd better tell Lieutenant Ayres."

"I don't think I'll help him a bit," Mrs. Strickland objected. "He wouldn't tell me what kinds of poisons they used for murders in Jeffersonian times. I asked him when he was trying to question me, and he was hardly even polite about it. I may want to murder one or two of my characters to get them out of the way," she added thoughtfully.

"I know what you mean," I agreed. The thought of Lieutenant Ayres's face when she asked him was almost too much. "But it might help Mr. Hawes and his wife instead of Lieutenant Ayres. So why don't you tell Dopey anyhow?"

"All right." She saw the justice of that. "Next time I see him."

Maude Ruskin came onto the platform then, and we stopped talking. She had some interesting things to say, in her businesslike way, about how agents help writers. Remembering that Mel had mentioned she was Mr. Gillespie's agent, I wondered if Lieutenant Ayres had consulted her about things in his past that might fit in with murder. No doubt he had. I'd better ask Mr. Bridgewater. I made a note to do that.

That phone booth of Mrs. Strickland's off the lobby turned out to be a real find for overhearing conversations. I was in it trying to locate Mr. Bridgewater (but I didn't get him) just before lunch, and Miss Ruskin unexpectedly turned up there beside it talking to Hamlyn Brent. I hadn't grasped that she was his agent too, though now I remembered that he had said he and Mr. Gillespie had the same agent and went to the same cocktail parties.

She said, "Darlin', I haven't mentioned it, of course, but you realize I know, don't you?" It was the impersonal "darlin'," not the affectionate one; I understood that.

"I'm sure you know everything, Maude," Mr. Brent conceded with that ironic overtone of his. "But which facet of knowledge is this specific bit?"

"You realize I couldn't handle Gil and you for so many years and not begin to realize what was going on, dear, and even when it started—about a year ago?" she said. "I just wanted you to know the bit is safe with me. Of course I know you didn't kill him, darlin'—I know you too well. But that policeman might think it if he knew. I'm just glad you can begin to produce again now—that's all I wanted to say. Under your own byline."

They went off then, and I came out of the booth wiping my hot face. So Hamlyn Brent, I deduced, is now going to be writing as John Smith? And what, if anything, has that to do with the murder of Carlton Gillespie? Maybe I'll ask him a few pointed questions in the workshop session this afternoon, I promised myself.

It was a lively session. He had asked for ways to make the women into murderers in a killing that required a man's strength, and the Writers had come up with everything from the obvious accomplice (her son in Mrs. Gillespie's case; her husband in Mrs. Hawes's) to lovely bits like drugging or poisoning him beforehand to make it easy to strangle and bash him, or having him bitten by a poisonous snake in the garden and already dying when the murderess began smashing him on the millstone. Miss DeBrett had brewed a concoction of deadly nightshade for him and had given it to him in an old-fashioned, which seemed to be her idea of a suitably labeled drink—indeed the only one—for a maiden lady with Inspirational Leanings to know about. She seemed to think an old-fashioned is made with lavender water and Queen Anne's lace and a sprig of mint.

I didn't like any of these wild ideas; I wanted something more subtle. Besides, none of these fitted in with the nether-millstone verse. But in the back of my head that matter of livelihood did faintly connect in some way with what Miss Ruskin had been saying to Hamlyn Brent.

I asked him innocently about pseudonyms for mystery writers; did he think an unusual pen name was a help? Yes, he thought so; it kept the readers more aware of the author's books as they came out; they recalled the name easily if they had liked the first one, and recognized it when they were looking for something new to read.

"Then there wouldn't be any reason for a writer with —say—a really super name like yours, which is well known to mystery fans, to change over suddenly to a more ordinary name?" I asked him.

"Of course not. Why would he?"

"I was just wondering," I said. He had never mentioned in the workshop that his real name was John Smith, but then there was no real reason he should. It wasn't a secret, I guessed; at any rate, it wasn't a secret to the police now. Probably lots of people knew it, the knowledgeable who kept up with the literary scene on a national scale, but the characters here wouldn't be likely to have run across such obscure information as the real names of writers who had used only their pen names for years.

"Are you considering a pen name, Miss Clark?" he asked with that maddening note of faint amusement.

"Yes," I said daringly. "Only I was thinking that perhaps for a mystery writer a name with a hint of alias about it might be intriguing. Like—John—Doe." I had started to say John Smith, but at the last minute my nerve failed.

"I think that would be cute," Miss DeBrett said.

"It really would," Mr. Brent agreed ironically. His eyes met mine, and now the amusement in them seemed tinged with a certain measuring thoughtfulness. A small chill touched the back of my neck. But I told myself *no*. And then I told myself even more sternly to please stop trying to provoke him.

"Let's get back to the mysterious women in murder mysteries," Mr. Brent said. "In one of my things, I remember, I had a woman as the killer when it seemed an impossible crime for a woman to commit. As in the old rule I told you about, all the possible solutions were eliminated, so it had to be the impossible one: the woman killed him. I don't recommend my twist, though, even though the story sold. It really was hardly fair to the reader—but then, I *had* planted plenty of indications all through the story."

"How? How did she—" the Writers clamored.

"She was a man in disguise," Mr. Brent explained. "But of course"—he tried to get us back on the subject—"there's no such possibility in the Gillespie case. There's no woman in the group of possible suspects—or even among the onlookers—who could be a man in disguise. You'll have to think of another gimmick, Miss Clark. So will the lieutenant."

"I probably won't let it be one of the women who's the murderer in my book," I said contrarily. "I'm going to use that Bible verse as the significant thing. The killing's going to have something to do with the victim threatening the murderer's livelihood. Or vice versa—revenge for the murderer's doing it to him. Maybe to get out of his clutches." I wondered if that would draw any return fire from Mr. Brent; he didn't know I had heard what Miss Ruskin said to him, of course, about his beginning to produce again now that Gil was dead.

But he remained imperturbable. "Well, can you outline it by tomorrow and bring it in for the group's criticism?" he suggested. Ah, yes, I thought, you'd like to see what I figure out along those lines, wouldn't you?

But I still didn't consider him a serious suspect. Not until later.

When I went through the lobby, I saw Dory Pevlin standing by a post smoking a cigarette and scowling as though the nicotine were eating his lungs out already.

"Hello. Haven't they arrested you yet?" I said flippantly, figuring that if they could've pinned it on him they already would have.

"They can't arrest me for wishing I'd killed him," Dory answered moodily. "Though—wait a minute! Do you suppose it's possible? Do you think I *could* have killed him by mental concentration? Suppose my astral body went out of my real body and *it* strangled him and beat his head in with all the fury of the way I felt about him—the way I would have liked to kill him, with no weapon but my bare hands—Yes! That's an excellent idea," he said with enthusiasm, and he looked more cheerful than I had ever seen him look before.

"It won't do for my book," I said. "Nobody's proved

yet that it's possible to kill somebody *in absentia.* But you could use it in a science fiction story," I suggested. "You could let it happen in a place called Absentia."

"Story!" he said scornfully. "It may be true, woman! Just because it hasn't been proved doesn't mean it's not possible. The Death Wish—not for yourself but for someone else. Have you no faith in the power of mind over matter? Dr. Rhine proved that psychokinesis can be demonstrated. Ever hear of dermographia?"

"I never heard of psycho—whatever even," I said frankly. "What is it?"

"It means that a force of the mind—apart from the physical brain—can produce a physical effect on an object. It's well-known in parapsychology. If I could think it with enough power, I could make you float through the air— that sort of thing. There was a woman in Paris once—this is a proved case—who could by the effort of her mind make a letter or a number appear on the skin of a person at a distance from her. That's dermographia. I suspect in some unenlightened times they called it witchcraft, too. If that can happen, who can say I might not have killed Gillespie when I wasn't anywhere near him?" The prospect seemed to make him very happy.

"Let me know when you go to explain that theory to Lieutenant Ayres," I said. "I'd like to see him flip. Aren't you at all sorry for Mr. Gillespie's family?" I asked curiously. "I understand his wife and daughter are all broken up about it."

"They're far better off without him," Dory said callously. "Why, you have only to read the stuff he wrote to tell the kind of person he was. A writer reveals himself

131

absolutely in his writing—didn't you know that? That's why analysts want to read what you've written. Three analysts have read everything I ever wrote."

"What do they make of it?" I asked curiously.

"They all think I'm putting them on," he said disdainfully. "But they aren't *critics.*"

"That's an idea, though," I suddenly realized, with a certain excitement. "I'd forgotten about his other writings. They might have a clue in them, too."

"What are you talking about?"

"Carlton Gillespie's stuff. On the table over there. I've got to go and read it. See you later."

There were three slick magazines with recent Gillespie novels in them—one a murder mystery. I took them and the Forrester Prize volume over to a nearby chair and started to read. I read the prize series first, because it was shorter.

It was an exciting exposé-type series which showed a great deal of enterprising work on the part of the crusading reporter, to uncover the Communist activities in various plants all over the state, including airplane factories. But I couldn't see how it could possibly tie in with any present-day motive for murder. Not like the Kay Hawes thing—no.

Then as I mused over it I caught a name among those who were being investigated as alleged Communists as a result of the exposé. It rang a faint bell. Which pen name, here at the conference, was the writing name of the man whose real name was Fitzgerald Mayo?

I couldn't remember to save my life which one it was. I tried to recall the names Mr. Bridgewater had mentioned from that list of his, but only the absurd Quinch and John Smith stuck with me—and Ellen Burpitt of course—though I had written them into my first draft when I was half asleep, from notes I took when he was telling me. But I knew I'd only have to look in my notes or ask Mr. Bridgewater.

With quick excitement I considered whether or not to glance through the magazine novels now or save them until later and go and find out about Fitzgerald Mayo right then. I couldn't hold out against my intense curiosity.

Why, this was another character with a motive for murder, if an innocent man branded as a Communist and "investigated" had resented it all these years. He might—he probably had—yes, he *must*—have lost his job because of it. The nether millstone—

The magazines could wait. I couldn't. I had to find out who Fitzgerald Mayo was.

9

Later on Wednesday Afternoon

I was starting to go up to my room to get my book notes when I glimpsed Mr. Bridgewater crossing the lobby. I hurried and caught up with him.

"Hello, Mr. Bridgewater. You're back from headquarters? Where are you going now?"

"Just down to the scene of the crime to take a look around since they moved the millstone," he said.

"I'll go with you. They took it down to headquarters, huh? I want to know what you found out—and I've got a new idea, and I need to ask you something."

"Why, all right, Libby." He looked flattered.

The police had finished looking for their clues in the garden; they had combed the grass thoroughly, and the hole where the millstone had been no longer attracted the curious. So the garden was deserted, looking almost as beautiful as it did day before yesterday, if you didn't count the hideous bare space where the old stone had lain before it became the Murder Instrument.

"Have you still got that list of pen names?" I asked as we sat down on the most secluded bench.

"Sure I have, Libby." Mr. Bridgewater searched through a number of odd scraps of paper and written-on envelopes in his pocket, muttering, "I know I had it right here someplace—" and finally found it. "Here."

I scanned it hurriedly: It wasn't easy to read his handwriting, especially after it had rubbed noses with the rest of the junk Mr. Bridgewater toted around in his pockets. "Van Saylor! I should have guessed—"

"What about him?"

"He's Fitzgerald Mayo. It's *another* motive for the murder, from out of the past. He was one of the alleged Communists that Mr. Gillespie exposed in the Forrester Prize series. He was 'investigated,' and he probably lost his job. Mr. Gillespie took his 'nether millstone,' don't you see? So if he were the least bit twisted in his mind and had been bitter about it all these years, he might have come here with revenge on his mind—reading in the paper that Carlton Gillespie was to be here in a triumphant appearance—yes, and he told me he had once lived in Birmingham, too. It all fits. They might have quarreled and he might have lost his temper and battered Mr. Gillespie—"

"Could be," Mr. Bridgewater said. "That about him being a Communist years ago was one of the things Dawson told me they'd gotten from New York. But he quit the party—he said—and hasn't been involved with it since."

"Anything else interesting in Sergeant Dawson's stuff?"

"Not very much. Writers don't generally have police records. They did turn up that Mr. Brent has been having money troubles for some time back home in New York. Seems he has two former wives demanding money all the time, almost getting him for contempt of court several times. But the ladies didn't even know Mr. Gillespie, as far as the boys could find out, so it doesn't connect."

"Well, it might if we could find out that he had the nether millstone around *his* neck. Mr. Brent, I mean. And that Mr. Gillespie had put it there." I realized then that my unconscious play on words was a real sure-enough mixed metaphor, but Mr. Bridgewater doesn't dig mixed metaphors. "Suppose he was the man on the phone who owed Mr. Gillespie money? They knew each other."

"He doesn't look much like the type to get all het up and kill a man with his bare hands," Mr. Bridgewater objected shrewdly, and even though he had never taken Psychology 7, I had to agree with him. Mr. Brent didn't look it, for a fact. He looked more like the exotic-poison-in-rare-wine type, who might kill his victim with a toast and a barbed epigram.

"Well, I'm going to see what I can pin on him when I have time," I said. "But right now let's go find Van Saylor and see what he has to say."

"Whoa—" Mr. Bridgewater put a hand on my arm. "I better phone Dopey Ayres and let him come and do the questioning, Libby. If Mr. Saylor *should* be the murderer, he could be dangerous if he thinks we know—"

"You've got a gun, haven't you?" I said hardily, challenging his male ego.

"Yeah—but I ain't shot at anybody in twenty years."

"Look, if Lieutenant Ayres comes to question Mr. Saylor, he won't even let me *be* there. This is something I found out—with your help, of course. We put two and two together ourselves. And I want us to follow it up ourselves, on account of my book I'm writing. If it turns out to be really anything, you can call Lieutenant Ayres fast."

"If I'm still alive," Mr. Bridgewater said grimly, "and able to talk. You don't know murderers, Libby. Best let the police handle 'em. I don't want you to get hurt."

"You *are* the police, Mr. Bridgewater." I coaxed and flattered. "He wouldn't resist you. And he wouldn't hurt me. He likes me. He's been making passes at me ever since the first day of the conference. Oh, not really, of course. Just in there trying."

"We-ell . . ." Mr. Bridgewater gave in. I knew he would. As we went back to the center to look for Van Saylor, I remembered to ask him, "Do you know if Lieutenant Ayres has found out from Ms. Ruskin anything significant about Mr. Gillespie's past as an author? She's his agent."

"He didn't when he first questioned her. He found out she was Gillespie's agent, yes, but she didn't know anything that seemed to have any connection with his murder. I don't think he's questioned her again."

"Well, we'll do that, too. When we have time. Or maybe I could get more out of her by myself. Since she's not likely to be dangerous." I smiled at him with a warmth calculated to make him feel protective, and he beamed. They ought to have lots of women in detective bureaus. I bet they could find out plenty—at least from male suspects.

It was getting on toward suppertime. Frank was at the desk, and I asked him if he'd seen Van Saylor around.

"Just went up," Frank said. "But you need an escort if you're going up to that old wolf's room, Libby."

"Mr. Bridgewater's going with me," I told him. "But just why do you think I can't handle one simple man?"

He grinned. "I guess you can. Especially since it's Miss Westover he's turned onto now. He's been panting after her, tongue hanging out, tail wagging, ever since Mr. Gillespie's been out of her picture."

"I'm younger and stronger than Miss Westover, and I have more resistance. It must be my antibodies, see? I used to be a Girl Scout, too. Resourceful. Prepared for any emergency, in the woods or out. Carry a Girl Scout ax and a knife with forty-five extra tools on my belt. Figuratively speaking."

"If Mr. Saylor's found dead, I'll tell them to look for those weapons."

Mr. Bridgewater didn't care much for this sophomoric banter. "Come on, Libby, let's get it over with," he said. He managed to make the elevator work after a few tries. He didn't exactly cuss it, because he respects Southern Womanhood. Especially mine.

We knocked at Van Saylor's door.

"Wait a minute—" Then he came to the door, still settling his shirt tail inside his belt.

"Well, this *is* a surprise! Libby! Come in. And Mr. Bridgewater." His voice allowed that he'd just as soon dispense with Mr. Bridgewater. "What'll you have to drink? I've got bourbon and Scotch—I was just going to have one before supper. I even got some ice."

"We can't stop for a drink, thanks, Mr. Saylor." It was awkward trying to explain what we had come for, when he was trying to make it a social occasion. "We want to ask you about something."

"If it's in my category, sure. But—it must be about the murder?" He looked at Mr. Bridgewater questioningly. "That's hardly in my category."

I answered. "You know I'm doing a mystery novel with this case as a base? Well, I don't set myself up as a detective or anything like that. But I find out anything I can that will help with the book. I've run across a few little things around here that Lieutenant Ayres hasn't had the opportunity—yet—to discover. One of them concerns you." I paused to give him time to look startled, but he didn't. "It seems to give you a possible motive for killing Mr. Gillespie. Of course we don't think you *did*," I hurried to say. I had just discovered that it is almost impossible to accuse an acquaintance of murder, to his face. "But we wanted you to explain it. Then if there's no reason to clutter up Lieutenant Ayres's mind with it while he's busy with more likely suspects, why, he doesn't have to know anything about it. So—will you tell us, just unofficially?" I looked at him with conscious appeal, realizing that I was being less than direct, but not quite sure how to put it over otherwise.

If he *was* a murderer, I thought then, he ought to be on the stage instead. Or a professional poker player. He showed not the slightest sign of perturbation. "Motive?" he said. "I don't think I ever saw the man before Sunday night, Libby. I'm not worried about your little spot-check, sweetheart. But I *am* curious. I didn't kill him. Why do you think I might have?"

"Have you forgotten," I said slowly, "the Forrester

Prize series he wrote? Can you still say you never saw him before? Your name—your real name—is among those exposed, investigated as possible Communists."

"Oh, that!" He walked away to the window, stood there staring out a minute—considering what to say?—then came back to us.

"I could stand on the Fifth Amendment," he suggested, with—could it be amusement?—in his voice. Did he turn his back because he was *laughing?* "But I won't. I'm not a Communist. All that's so long ago. I admit when I was younger I thought there might be something in it. But I found out better. I quit the fellow-traveler stuff. I'm a Liberal, yes, but not a Communist. Can't you tell I'm not the least bit mad about that old lie? I'm not even the same man I was then. I've never had much respect for Carlton Gillespie—for various reasons—but I didn't care enough about what he did to kill him for it. And I never met him face to face at all."

He sounded very convincing, careless of whether we believed him or not.

"Besides," he went on casually, "if I *were* going to hate anybody about that story, Carlton Gillespie wasn't the one to hate. He didn't dig up that stuff. He just did the office rewrite and got the byline and accepted the Forrester Prize for the exposé. That's one reason I didn't have much respect for him. But I can't even remember the name of the reporter who really did the job of exposing. You see how little I cared, how little I hated."

He had made out a good case—a surprising case. But I was going to check it.

"Well, thanks, Mr. Saylor," I said, standing up and hurrying Mr. Bridgewater. "What you say sounds reasonable. I don't see any need to bother Lieutenant Ayres about it just now, do you, Mr. Bridgewater?"

"No. Guess not."

"Sure you won't have a drink?" Van Saylor said, still sounding amused. "Now that you don't think you'd be drinking poison? With a murderer?"

"I didn't think that," I assured him. "But we really haven't time. We've got to see some other people before supper."

"More suspects?" He laughed, seeing us to the door. "Libby, I hope your book's a best seller. You're working mighty hard on it. I'd like to see you sometime when you aren't working. Just—socially."

"Sure," I said vaguely. "A *blind* date." That ought to get through to him by next week, I thought. That sports coat! The door closed on his slightly bewildered look.

"What did you mean by that, Libby?" Mr. Bridgewater asked.

"I'd have to be blind," I explained, and he laughed and said, "I get it." At last.

I pursued: "Let's see Mrs. Gillespie and ask her if that story of his could possibly be the truth."

"Good idea. Ought to be checked." He puffed after me as I hurried around the corner to the corridor where my room and the Gillespies' room were.

Mel opened the door when we knocked. His mother sat in the armchair, her face pale but composed. The girl in the other chair, a pretty blonde who looked a lot like Mel and Mrs. Gillespie and fortunately not at all like her father, had obviously been crying. For a long time. Carla, of course.

"Well, come in," Mel said cordially. "Hi, Libby. Hi,

Mr. Bridgewater. Mother, you know Libby Clark. And, Carla, I'd like for you and Libby to be friends. My sister. Mother, this is Mr. Bridgewater."

I spoke to Mrs. Gillespie, trying to make "How are you?" full of sympathy and condolence.

She couldn't smile, but she said, "Won't you sit down, both of you?"

We sat on the bed. Hospital rooms and hotel rooms never have enough chairs. I sat close to Carla's chair and leaned over and said to her impulsively, "I know how you feel. I'm so sorry." For you, I added mentally. Not exactly because Carlton Gillespie was murdered—I couldn't care less about that—but because someone you loved is dead. And I thought again of my dad, and decided to call home tonight. I did, too, before I began writing this.

Carla started crying again, covering her face with her hands. I could barely understand what she was saying in that muffled, forlorn voice. "No matter what Mel says, I'm going to find out who killed him—no matter who it was—" Whom did she suspect, then? Her mother and Mel?

So Mel must have been foolish enough to tell her something of why he thought Mr. Gillespie was no great loss, perhaps even—rashly—that he deserved killing. He should have waited. He didn't have to add to her grief, poor girl.

"I do know how you feel," I said again. "If it were my father—" I wanted to put my arms around her and be sympathetic, but I didn't know how. And I wanted to say something consoling to Mrs. Gillespie, but the words wouldn't come. Mr. Bridgewater was saying he was sorry, though.

142

Finally I said, "I feel so sad for you," which was a pretty good compromise. Then, sort of losing my nerve about asking his mother questions at that point, I said to Mel, "Mr. Bridgewater and I wanted to ask you something. Could you come with us for a few minutes?"

"Sure. I'll be right back, Mother."

A few more murmurs of vague condolence, and we were in the corridor. "Mel," I said, "does your mother know I'm writing about all this as my book project?"

"You didn't mind that I told her, did you?" Mel said. "When I asked her if you could see the proofs, I had to tell her why. She says she doesn't mind, but I guess she doesn't realize—well, anyhow, it probably won't get published, will it?"

"Well, now I know what you think of my writing," I said.

"Aw, Libby, I didn't mean—you know I didn't. Why, I've never even read any of your writing."

"Never mind. You could've if you'd wanted to." I smiled, so he'd know I wasn't really annoyed, and confided then. "Mr. Bridgewater and I ran across something today that we wanted to ask your mother about, but then I got cold feet when I saw how upset Carla was. But it might be important if the murder is ever to get solved —so do you suppose she'd understand if I went on and asked her now, even when I—and everybody—really ought to let her alone?"

"Why don't I go and ask her?" Mel said. He was the direct sort, and of course he wouldn't have any delicacy about his mother's feelings toward the stepfather he despised. He didn't care, so naturally he wouldn't have any insight into how deeply she might care. And Carla.

143

He came back to say his mother would try to tell me what I wanted to know, and added, "And Carla was all for it when I said you thought it might be important in finding out who killed Gil."

"You're nice, Mel. And so are they. I really hate to ask questions now—I was sorry when Lieutenant Ayres bothered her. But it might even help Carla—to think somebody's trying—even if it is for a different reason. Well, anyhow, thanks, Mel."

Mr. Bridgewater just put a hand on Mel's shoulder as we followed him back into the room.

I didn't feel comfortable about it, though, until Mrs. Gillespie said, "It's all right, Libby. The police don't seem to be very much interested in finding out who might have —wanted to kill Gil." She spoke wearily, but as though she were accustomed to doing things that would please Mel, and she thought he wanted her to be nice to me. "What is it?"

I found I could look her in the face, after all. "Maybe the police are trying," I said. "But they don't know what we just discovered, and we hardly know whether to tell them or not. Maybe you can help us decide. You see, we found out that 'Van Saylor' is the pen name of Fitzgerald Mayo—a man who was exposed as a possible fellow-traveler in your husband's Forrester Prize series and 'investigated.' Lost his job on account of it. That seemed like a good motive for murder—if he had a twisted mind and had been brooding about it all these years. The nether millstone, you see?

"But Mr. Bridgewater and I just talked to Mr. Saylor, and he talked himself out of that corner—if *you* can remember whether what he says is true or not. Mrs. Gillespie, he says he couldn't have been bitter toward your husband about it, because Mr. Gillespie wasn't the reporter who did the actual work on that series. He says another reporter dug up all the facts, and Mr. Gillespie just wrote the stories in the office, as a rewrite man. He can't remember the reporter's name, even, so he says that proves he didn't care enough to commit murder about it after all these years. Mrs. Gillespie, can you remember back to when the series first came out? Do you think what Van Saylor says could possibly be true? *Could* some other reporter have done the work?"

Mrs. Gillespie sat silent for a moment, then she nodded slowly. "I suppose I shouldn't say so, now that he's—dead," she said. "But there comes a time for truth. . . . Yes. I never understood why he would do things like that. He had plenty of talent and ability himself—he didn't *need* to take credit for work somebody else had done. But—he did. I remember his laughing about the Forrester Prize series, as if it were a big joke that the prize had gone to the wrong writer. At first, you see, when it wasn't a question of the prize, the byline wasn't important. The other reporter who dug up the facts and exposed them should have shared it, by rights, but Gil was the fair-haired-boy with the paper's brass just then, and the city editor was probably just pleasing them by giving Gil the single byline. Later, when the series won the Forrester Prize, Gil didn't have enough of what it takes to say he didn't deserve it. He accepted the prize. So—yes, Mr. Saylor's story is true."

I had known it was, all the time, I told myself. So—he

had taken other things besides Kay Warden's poem. Kay —could *she* have been the other reporter who did the digging? A crusading girl reporter—the chauvinist males on the staff wouldn't have minded that a girl didn't get credit for her work. She had been on the paper at the time. She would at least have known about it.

"Do you remember"—my voice would hardly come out, I was so breathless with excitement—"who the other reporter was, Mrs. Gillespie?"

"No. He never said. He laughed about it, about how stupid the Forrester Prize judges were, but he actually thought deep down in his heart that he deserved it more than the other reporter—because of the way he wrote it, you see, his famous 'style.' He could always manage to justify to himself anything he wanted to do."

She spoke with some bitterness, and I thought she was not talking wholly of his writing.

Carla gasped out, "You're not fair to him—you shouldn't talk like that! He was a great writer—"

"Yes," her mother said somberly, repeating, "he didn't *need* to steal other people's work. It was just some strange flaw in him—" And I thought of mental kleptomania. I must ask Dory Pevlin if there is such a thing. Surely one of his three analysts might have mentioned it.

"But—the other reporter?" I kept on trying. "Could it —Mrs. Gillespie, think if it could have been Kay Hawes? Kay Warden *then?*"

She thought about that for a long moment, trying probably to remember if there was anything he had ever said that would indicate whether the reporter was a woman or not. But Gil, of course, would have been wary of bringing up Kay's name at all. If it was Kay, that part hadn't been in *The Passionate Circumstance.* At least not as far as I had read, and that covered her active newspaper days. But then, he wouldn't have been likely to include something as unflattering to his hero as that bit. He wouldn't have, even disguised as fiction.

"I suppose it could," she said at last. "Why don't you ask her?"

"I will if she ever shows up," I promised. I remembered that I hadn't checked lately to see if she had come home. "They think she ran away, you know. But Mel told you last night."

"Yes. I'm—sorry."

Carla was crying hard again, fighting against what she must have known were the harsh facts about her father, but were in conflict with the tender side he somehow had to have shown her.

I thought, it would give Kay another motive—if she needed another motive. But if she didn't kill him or encourage Professor Hawes to, then she won't mind saying if she was the one who did the work on that series—and maybe *let* Gil take the credit and the prize because she loved him. Yes. There would have had to be some reason why the one who did the real work didn't protest when Gil got the prize.

I realized, by the way Mrs. Gillespie looked, that the truth about *The Passionate Circumstance* could have already filtered through to her, and I thought we'd better leave.

"Anyone who was on the paper at the time would probably remember," she said tiredly. "It was probably talked about. There's a rapid turnover on that paper, I understand, but there still are surely a few old-timers left—"

"The police could check, easily," I agreed. "But I'm going to ask Mrs. Hawes first, if I can, before I let Lieutenant Ayres in on it. Maybe it won't have to come out, if it doesn't turn out to be what they call 'the motive.' Thanks, Mrs. Gillespie, for being so patient. And Mel. Carla—" I was so sorry for her, I couldn't even say anything else. Mr. Bridgewater beat me to the door.

But I couldn't ask Kay Hawes about anything. Ever. Because later on that evening they found her, and she had been dead for more than twenty-four hours.

10

Wednesday Evening

Mrs. Strickland found her, to be exact.

The Summer School Theater's play (*Our American Cousin,* just as the Ford Theater had put it on, of all things), was to have been given in the auditorium, for the conference tonight, and Mrs. Strickland got there early, as usual. She's too nearsighted to see a clock, but yesterday when I kidded her about being early for everything she got miffed and insisted that her watch keeps perfect time— that her jeweler who regulates it is the one who keeps the railroad men's watches accurate. And she had even forgotten to put it on after her bath, anyhow! Maybe she's just subconsciously impatient for things to start happening.

They did, all right. As usual, too, she had to go to the rest room. For some reason the maid hadn't yet unlocked the regular lounge, and Mrs. Strickland, who wasn't backward about poking around, went backstage hunting for the actors' rest rooms. Nobody had been using the dressing-rooms here for some time; the Summer Theater actors rehearsed in their own theater at the other end of the campus, and only a few of them had arrived by this time for tonight's performance.

Mrs. Strickland found the rest rooms, all right, and she wished she hadn't. She screamed almost loud enough for Lieutenant Ayres to hear her down at headquarters. He got there before I did, at that. I hurried over there as soon as Frank told me they'd found Mrs. Hawes. The lieutenant and all the rest of the crew, the cops and detectives, the photographer and the fingerprint man and Dr. Mabie and the ambulance intern and the reporters and all, were already there. Lieutenant Ayres was asking Mrs. Strickland to explain why she went to that particular rest room, and she was blushing dark red and trying to tell him it was the same reason that anybody goes to a rest room, only the other one wasn't open.

They had the whole backstage shut off and wouldn't let anybody go near this time, so I didn't see Mrs. Hawes's body. I'm sort of glad I didn't. But Mrs. Strickland told me about it later. She said Kay looked perfectly dreadful. She had been choked to death by somebody's bare hands, too, Mrs. Strickland said in a hushed, awestruck voice. Mr. Bridgewater later told me Dr. Mabie's tentative conclusion: she'd been dead since between three and five o'clock Tuesday afternoon. And they suspected poor Professor Hawes of killing her—his own wife—because she could have found out that he killed Mr. Gillespie on her account. Absurd, masculine-type reasoning, of course. No woman would have accepted it.

They made him a definite suspect because of a tactical blunder on his part. Sometimes I think nearly all men are dumb. He was so upset about her disappearance that he evidently couldn't think—and instead of burning those galleys he got when he came to my room last night, he waited to read them. Lieutenant Ayres had gone out to his house to question him again about his wife's disappearance and had noticed the proofs. Mr. Hawes hadn't even hidden them.

Lieutenant Ayres naturally thought it strange that Mr. Hawes should have been reading the galleys of Mr. Gillespie's book just at this time and decided to read them himself. The lieutenant's no fool; he didn't have much trouble putting two and two together into a triangle. Mrs. Strickland had told him about overhearing Mrs. Hawes ask the Professor if he killed Mr. Gillespie and hearing him deny it. But the lieutenant said that indicated Mrs. Hawes didn't kill Mr. Gillespie herself, all right, but it proved nothing at all about Mr. Hawes except that a man could lie to his wife if he had a good reason to.

So now, Mr. Bridgewater said, they were seriously considering arresting Professor Hawes. After all, they had to arrest somebody soon.

"Oh, no! That's cruel," I protested. "If you could have seen him when he talked to me last night, Mr. Bridgewater, you'd *know* how much he loved her. He didn't kill her. Or Mr. Gillespie. Oh, those poor children of theirs—"

"Mrs. Dawson's gone over to help with the kids," Mr. Bridgewater said. "We don't think he did it, either, Libby.

151

And Dopey will find it out, give him time enough. You got woman's intuition to help you figure things out, but Dopey ain't got a thing to help him except police investigation."

Mr. Bridgewater said Lieutenant Ayres wanted to establish when was the last time anybody saw Mrs. Hawes alive. I realized now that I probably saw her shortly before she was killed, if it happened nearer three than five P. M. "I saw her not long before the three-thirty workshop," I told him. "Mr. Phillips and I had just come out of the auditorium, and she was going back there to—yes, Mr. Hawes mentioned last night that she was going back to the auditorium to look for a pen she lost, the last time he saw her. She spoke to me and to Mr. Phillips, and I didn't actually see her go in, but of course she must have. I went on toward the center. There wasn't anybody at all left in the auditorium when we came out." I remembered that. "Unless someone was hiding in there—of course that's possible. Or of course anybody could have gone in after she did."

"If he knew she was going back in there—back to look for her pen," Mr. Bridgewater said significantly. "At least, that's what Dopey will think about Professor Hawes."

"They're not putting on the play tonight, are they?" I said. "Though of course I wouldn't put it past Dean Crossett to try."

"No," Mr. Bridgewater said. "There's too much excitement for that. I guess Dopey will have to question all of you-all again."

He did, too, and the workshops accounted for almost everybody's whereabouts after three-thirty, but not between three and three-thirty. Nobody could pinpoint seeing Mr. Hawes at that time, according to Mr. Bridgewater. Nobody had seen Mel Alston or Hamlyn Brent or Van Saylor or Dory Pevlin, either.

I met Dory as I was leaving the inquisition. "Hi," I said. "Do you think you could have killed *her* by remote control?"

"No," he said dazedly, wandering on. The fact that murder was an ugly thing to strike anyone except Carlton Gillespie seemed to have come home to him suddenly. He wouldn't have wanted to kill Kay Hawes.

But no one would have wanted to, I found myself pondering. She wasn't somebody like Carlton Gillespie, whom half a dozen people would have been glad to see dead. There's simply nobody who would have had any reason to kill *her.* Unless—she knew something that pointed to the murderer, that put him in danger of discovery. She had told Professor Hawes she knew what the Bible verse meant. Could the murderer have found out that she did? Yes, if she could put the finger on somebody—knowingly or not—that would be the reason she was killed. But it wasn't her husband who killed her, I was sure.

Mrs. Strickland and Mrs. Nelson came along with me to the coffee shop. They had already been questioned, and Mrs. Nelson had to have another drink for her nerves. She got her usual ice and poured it on, Mrs. Strickland got her hot coffee, and I had a Coke. Everybody was there (except Professor Hawes); I thought, glancing around, that if any of them should need an alibi for this particular time, I could supply it. At the next table even the unhappy Mr. Phillips was having a Coke, with—or without—Dory Pev-

153

lin. Dory was just sitting there. Mr. Saylor and Mr. Brent were sitting with them too, probably because the place was crowded. It certainly wasn't because any of them felt sociable. None of them was saying a word.

"Just think," Mrs. Strickland said with awe, "she was there, dead and staring like that, all the time Ms. Ruskin was talking this morning. She was there by herself all night—"

"She was there while poor Professor Hawes was going out of his mind thinking she had run away," I said soberly. "And now—think how he's feeling now."

"He musht need a drink," Mrs. Nelson said. She was in a little deeper tonight than usual, I noticed; indeed you could say she was drunk, if you needed a blunt adjective. Her eyes weren't even focusing. "I jusht remembered," she said confidentially, but much too loud for confidences. "Couldn't 'member anything in there when he ashed me —I jusht 'membered, though. I saw her go into that audi-audi-torium, you know, and she met Paul—"

"Paul?" I said. "Paul who?"

"*You* know Paul," Mrs. Nelson said, waving her hand so that the drink in it slopped over onto the table. She wiped at it with exaggerated care, with her paper napkin, missing the wet place entirely. "She called 'im Paul. Paul —like in the Bible—'member? It wash Paul preached to the Co—" Her voice wavered; she was nearly falling over, asleep.

"Paul *who?*" I was getting impatient.

"Paul—Shaul—you know Shaul—" Mrs. Nelson's stream of consciousness was way off in the New Testament now; she wasn't in the present context at all, I concluded. Saul of Tarsus? Or was she just slurring her consonants again? Maybe she had changed her book's scene from the Old Testament to the New. But surely she wasn't going to abandon Moses and Miriam right there in the Pentateuch? I'd have to catch her early enough tomorrow to find out if Paul was a Biblical character in her book or a real person.

"I don't think Sophie saw Mrs. Hawes at all," Mrs. Strickland confided behind her hand. "I think she's just got it all mixed up with some of those Bible characters. She's—you know—had just a little too much."

"Probably you're right," I agreed. "She ought to go to bed." Mrs. Nelson didn't even realize we were talking about her. Her eyes were closing.

I saw Mel come in then and pause and look around. He started over toward us when he saw me. "Excuse me, girls," I said, getting up hastily. "There's my football player."

"Love'sh young dream," Mrs. Nelson mumbled indulgently.

Mrs. Strickland said, "You go right ahead, honey. We're going up to bed in a few minutes, but it doesn't matter how late it is, does it, when you're young. He's a good-looking boy. Something like my young Thomas Jefferson, you know, if only he weren't blond."

I steered Mel out of the crowded place and we looked for an unoccupied corner of the lobby. We found a secluded sofa behind a palm. I noticed in myself an odd reluctance to go out into the moonlight, even with Mel. I knew there was no danger, but the back of my neck didn't. My chilly spine didn't. Somewhere among us might be a murderer, and it was a horrid thing to realize. I had never before walked around in a company that included a probable murderer. I had never been afraid of the dark before, either. But I was now.

"Anything new?" I said.

"No. I just—I just wanted to see you." He sounded appealing, lonely and distressed about his mother and sister and needing sympathy. I was more than willing to give it to him, yet in the back of my consciousness there was still the caution that reminded me that *if* it was possible for Mel to be acting a part, and *if* he could have killed Mr. Gillespie and then killed Kay to keep from being found out, then he might have said just that, to soften me up so I'd go out into the night with him later. To act like Jack the Ripper, only using his strong hands instead of a knife. More like the Boston Strangler. I couldn't help studying Mel's hands. They *were* strong, I remembered.

But no. I drew a deep breath of relief as it struck me that he had come looking for me openly in a crowded place where lots of people had seen us go out together. No, Mel wasn't acting a part; he wasn't trying to lure me anywhere.

"What are you shaking your head for?" he asked curiously. "Don't you believe me?"

"You tell that to all the girls," I said lightly. You 'just wanted to see them.' "

"No. I'm beginning to realize it's you, Libby," he said earnestly. "I think I'm falling in love with you."

I didn't have time for a love affair right then, though I admit if I could have put my mind to it I might have been able to simmer up to the boiling point without a whole lot of trouble. We could have worked up a pretty wow relationship. Mel was very attractive. Maybe later, I promised myself, after I finish my book. Next semester.

"You're sweet," I said. "You remind me of a cub scout I used to go with when I was about eight. He said, so seriously, 'I think I'm falling in puppy love.' He gave me my first heart box of chocolates on Valentine's Day," I said dreamily. "And his cub scout ring."

"And what did you do?"

"I kissed him, of course."

"Like this?" He looked around swiftly and saw no one looking. It was a really perfect kiss, and I liked it quite a lot. But I knew I had to get on up to my room and write up all the things that have happened today.

So I unglued my lips from his and said, "And then we ate all the chocolates and felt pretty sick—not a bit romantic. . . . Do you think you can make that elevator work? I've got to get to work now on my book."

He didn't much want to, but he did.

So I've barricaded the doors again and caught up with the facts on the second murder. Tomorrow I'll find out, if I can, where Mr. Brent says he was between three and three-thirty yesterday afternoon (it's already A.M.). I remember how cool and calm he was about everything at the workshop at three-thirty, though, and a doubt bothers me. *Could* a man strangle a woman and not even appear strange at all, right afterward? Well, only if he was strange to begin with, sort of like—well, like Dory Pevlin, I find myself thinking.

And I just wrote myself a note to be sure to ask Nan Gorman about that phone call. I've been so busy today that I forgot about seeing her.

I *must* be going to be a murder mystery writer.

Because as soon as I wrote that down I thought, if she

did listen in, and did recognize the voice, and if the person did have anything to do with the murder, and if he finds out she knows—then Nan Gorman will be murdered too. Very soon. Nan Gorman may be the third victim. Tomorrow . . .

Or maybe she's already dead. Stuffed in a closet or rest room somewhere on this campus . . .

Then I slapped my lurid imagination down, resisting the impulse to phone Nan right now, late as it is. Of course she isn't the third victim. I'll be able to see her tomorrow without any trouble at all.

There isn't going to be any third victim.

Is there?

11

Thursday Morning and Afternoon

This morning, as soon as I'd had breakfast, I sat down and gave myself a few instructions, on paper. I realized I had to get better organized. I had to stop leaving loose ends all over the place, the way I'd been doing. I had to finish one train of thought and see where it led before I went flapping off on another one.

The loose ends I had left dangling yesterday were mainly Nan Gorman and the phone conversation, and the slick magazine novels of Carlton Gillespie, and checking very circumspectly with Maude Ruskin about Hamlyn Brent—if I could work up a conversation with her without its seeming too obvious. Maybe I could sign up for an individual conference with her about advising me whether or not to try to get an agent for my book, as so many of the writers were doing, and then lead her gradually into talking about other mystery writers.

I checked with Frank, and Nan wouldn't be on duty again until this afternoon. She's going to summer school, so was probably in a morning class. But Maude Ruskin had a few minutes free that she could give me right after Serena Wilcox's talk at 10:30 on women's magazine fiction, in the auditorium. Yes, Dean Crossett had talked the police into putting the auditorium back into use (all except the backstage section) after they had searched every inch of the place to try to decide exactly where Kay had been when she was strangled. They hadn't found a thing to point to any specific place, according to Mr. Bridgewater. He came up just as I was writing my name on the individual conference sheet on the bulletin board, for Miss Ruskin at 11:30.

He had no news, except that the reporters were about to drive Dopey Ayres crazy. "Poor Dopey keeps telling 'em it was only day before yesterday the whole thing started," he said. "Seems like it was longer ago than that, doesn't it? Dopey tries to explain that they couldn't expect an arrest yet, that it takes time to go through all the routine stuff, comparing fingerprints and checking backgrounds and checking one person's statement against another's and trying to fit all the details in place—"

"Don't I know it!" I said.

He confided that they hadn't actually arrested Professor Hawes yet, but they were keeping a man on his house. And they were watching several people here at the center too.

"Who?" I urged.

"You ain't supposed to know," he said. "Nobody's supposed to know. I ain't either."

"Tell me anyhow," I begged. "Is Mr. Brent one of them?"

"I can't say, Libby, much as I'd like to. They'd have Dawson's job if anything slipped up because of his telling me something that I let anybody else find out."

"Has Lieutenant Ayres been threatening you—or Officer Dawson?" I asked indignantly.

"'Course not." But he wouldn't tell me any more, except that Dopey thought this was a case of a sudden impulse to kill, not premeditated, because there was no Bible verse this time. He thought the two killings were connected, though, because both victims were strangled. Brilliant deduction.

Mr. Bridgewater said for me to be careful who I talked to, and not to go alone into *any* vacant place with *any*body, because he didn't want anything to happen to me like what happened to Kay Hawes. And maybe I knew too much, too.

"Don't worry," I assured him. "I'm going to skip Miss Wilcox's lecture this morning and sit right here in the lobby and read magazines."

"That's a good quiet thing to do," he agreed, and went off on his morning rounds.

It was quiet in one sense, but in another it was one of the most exciting mornings I've spent yet.

I read through Carlton Gillespie's two general magazine novels without finding a thing that could be applied to the events here. They were very ordinary novels, I thought; surely I ought to be able to get *my* stuff published if the magazines were that hard up. I had saved the mystery novel for last.

As I read through it—I'm a speed reader on light stuff

161

—my brain began to frown even before my forehead did. Something was wrong here. I had read this gimmick before somewhere. It was such a familiar twist—or— Wait! Now I remembered. I could hear the ironic voice saying, ". . . in one of my things, I remember, I had a woman as the killer when it seemed an impossible crime for a woman to commit. . . . All the possible solutions were eliminated, so it had to be the impossible one: the woman killed him. I don't recommend my twist, though. . . . It really was hardly fair to the reader—but then I *had* planted plenty of indications all through the story." And I could hear the collective soprano demand, "How?" and the ironic answer, "She was a man in disguise."

Here in Carlton Gillespie's "Cherchez l'Homme," his character, Martha Webster, who couldn't have killed Louis Raine because it required masculine strength, had just been unmasked as a man in disguise.

I sat there trying to figure it out. It was Mr. Brent's plot, no doubt about it. Carlton Gillespie, that mental kleptomaniac who shoplifted from other people's minds, had stolen another reporter's work for the Forrester Prize series. Maybe Kay Hawes's. He had stolen Kay Hawes's poem—and her secret—for his hardcover novel. And he had stolen Hamlyn Brent's work for this magazine mystery. How could he expect to get away with it this time? Maybe Mr. Brent had published it a very long time ago, and Mr. Gillespie thought nobody would remember the gimmick if he changed names and places and lots of other details. Or he could always claim coincidence if—

Or—wait. The telephone conversation came back to me, and my heart began to pound in my throat. Yes. That would explain it. *If* Hamlyn Brent was the man who owed

Mr. Gillespie money—and he well might be, owing so much to his ex-wives that he had gotten in deeper and deeper financially—yes, that was possible. On the phone Mr. Gillespie had referred to work the debtor had done for him—and a piece of work he had yet to do, or pay up. The man had very likely been protesting against doing any more of that work. Yes. Mr. Gillespie could have been forcing Hamlyn Brent to produce mystery stories for him, or plots at least. It would have been most repugnant to a man like Mr. Brent to do it. And he had simply slipped up and forgotten, when he told the workshop that plot, that the story was supposed to be Gillespie's.

That would explain, too, why Mr. Brent had appeared to have—what was it Van Saylor had said?—"written himself out." Why he hadn't recently been producing any murder mysteries of his own. The whole thing would have been intolerable. And Maude Ruskin had said that *now* he could produce under his own byline again. She hadn't meant "John Smith" instead of Hamlyn Brent, as I had assumed; she had meant "Hamlyn Brent" instead of "Carlton Gillespie."

Then I remembered the nether millstone, and I got excited all over again. It fitted so perfectly. Mr. Gillespie was taking Mr. Brent's livelihood away. And Mr. Brent was in the next room to mine. And the door between had been unlocked Monday evening until I locked it. He could have swapped the Bibles all right. He didn't have any alibi for around midnight that evening. He was strong enough to have killed Carlton Gillespie. If Nan had listened in and could identify him—or even make an independent guess before I suggested him—

But—the one thing that wasn't explained was the murder of Kay Hawes. True, Mr. Brent had nobody to confirm that he was in his room, as he had said he was, until time for the workshop. He had said, according to Mr. Bridgewater, that he had to walk up and down the stairs, on account of the elevator's balking, so nobody in the lobby saw him. The stairs come out on the side.

But as far as I could see, he had no reason for killing Mrs. Hawes. This new theory took the motive far from that newsroom in Birmingham. She couldn't have known anything about why Hamlyn Brent hated Carlton Gillespie—could she? And she wasn't even here at the center after the picnic was over that night. I had heard her say she was going home, so she couldn't have seen him killing Mr. Gillespie or even have seen him near the garden. Could she have found out something later—something incriminating—quite by accident?

Well, it was one possibility of innocence for Mr. Brent, I admitted. But there were so many possibilities of guilt that I actually dreaded the idea of going to his workshop this afternoon.

I put the magazines back on the table and went over to Frank. "What time does Nan come on this afternoon?" I asked, probably with my impatience showing.

"About four. If you're so anxious to talk to her, Libby, why don't you call her?"

"Won't do," I answered. "She won't tell me what I want to know, over the phone. Somebody else might listen in and know—Besides, with the wires in the shape they're in here, I might find myself talking to Lieutenant Ayres instead."

"Did the great detective get her wires crossed?" Frank

kidded, but I just wrinkled my nose at him and went on up to Ms. Ruskin's room. By stairs, naturally. It's a good thing I'm young and active.

Of course it wouldn't be any use to ask Nan anything on the phone. It would be hard enough to get her to admit to listening in if I urged her in person.

Well, I didn't get anywhere at all with Ms. Ruskin. She gave me a list of agents who will consider taking promising new writers, all right, but she said kindly that she herself has all the clients she can handle right now.

And then when I tried to get her to talk about those clients she's handling, she clammed up like an oyster, as Mrs. Strickland would say. I'm getting fonder and fonder of Mrs. Strickland. I think I'm going to enjoy her book even though *The Mistress* isn't meant to be a satire or the least bit humorous. She's promised to let me be the first to read it when she gets it finished.

"I've always liked Hamlyn Brent's murder stories so much," I said to Ms. Ruskin, acting as wide-eyed as I could. "You're his agent, aren't you, Ms. Ruskin? Why doesn't he bring out a new one? It's been so long since *The Alley Cat Murders.*"

"He probably will," she said calmly. "Very soon now. I think he's working on a new one. It should be excellent."

"But why hasn't he brought out anything for such a long time?" I persisted. "He used to do two a year."

"I don't know," she said blandly. "His editors would like the answer to that, too. Well, you try Cyrus Black when you get something ready for an agent to look at, Miss Clark. I hear he's taking a few beginners if they show talent."

"Thanks, Ms. Ruskin."

Lunch was unexciting. Mrs. Nelson evidently wasn't coming to lunch, I thought, and she hadn't been to Miss Wilcox's talk either, Mrs. Strickland reported; probably she had a bad hangover from last night. Nobody had seen her all day. She had been really lit, I mused. The drunkest I'd seen her in the three whole days. Talking all that stuff about Bible characters—and Kay Hawes—

Miss DeBrett told us she had decided to combine the Inspiration of *God's Garden* with the Practical Side, by including a few highlights of Japanese Flower Arranging, because her nephew had been in Japan during the Korean Trouble and could give her some Pointers. She was eating yogurt and carrots for lunch.

Mrs. Strickland had had another conference with Dr. Petersen, and he had convinced her that she should do a little more research on John Quincy Adams before she had him also in love with "The Mistress" in any *mature* way. "Dr. Petersen thinks—he's not sure, but he *thinks*—that young Adams was a boy of about seven at the time," she confided. "That might make him somewhat precocious. So I promised I'd look it up before I go any further with that particular bedroom scene." She's getting less bashful all the time.

As we left the dining room I managed to get away from the two ladies gracefully, but it wasn't easy. Not one of us was interested in Cobb Wilmer's talk in the auditorium on TV playwriting, and they wanted to talk about their own writing until workshop time, with anybody who'd listen. I thought it'd be just as well if they talked to each other; then neither would have to listen.

I saw Hamlyn Brent pause by the outside door to fit a

fresh unlit cigarette into his holder, and I came up beside him and said with playful but grim suddenness, "Where were you between three and three-thirty yesterday afternoon?"

He looked at me coolly. "Just write the stories, Miss Clark. You don't have to live them. Make up where I was. As a matter of fact, I was in my room. Alone. A man really needs to be gregarious, doesn't he, in a situation like this. So that he'll never be alone at a crucial time when he should have an alibi. Where were *you* between three and three-thirty yesterday afternoon?" he added derisively. "Kissing an athletic young man behind a potted palm?"

I flushed hotly; I could feel my face burning. So he had seen Mel kiss me last night, and he thought it goes on all the time. He must have come out of the coffee shop soon after I did. So what. I hadn't considered it a particularly athletic kiss, either. "I was in room two-oh-six with eleven other people waiting for you to arrive to conduct the mystery workshop. You were a little late," I said coldly. "I was polishing up a few notes on motives and opportunities centering around this puzzle we have here," I added significantly.

He laughed. "An excellent idea. Do keep on with it, Miss Clark."

I couldn't resist the temptation to see his reaction, though I realized in a moment that it might be dangerous —that again I'd given away something that might better not have been known. I said sweetly, "I was reading Mr. Gillespie's latest murder story this morning. It was very interesting."

He paused, for just a fraction of a second, with the door

half open—just long enough for what I said to catch up with him. Then he said, "Oh?" with detached politeness, and waited.

My move next. And I didn't know where to move. He was so cool about it all, so unlikely a person to strangle anybody. I couldn't think of another thing to say.

Mr. Brent smoothly let me off the hook. "That's right, Miss Clark," he said with only a trace of mockery. "A student of the genre can't read too many of the current murder mysteries. It's very good practice in learning what not to do when *you* write one." He smiled with Mephisto's own glee at me as he went on out the door, and I almost saw him curve a barbed tail suavely over his arm. I stood there stifling a few childish curses, thinking of the things I might have said if only I'd been a little bit quicker with the repartee.

Well, I'd go upstairs and see how old Sophie was getting along, I decided, while I waited for Nan to come on duty at the switchboard.

I knocked at Mrs. Nelson's door and listened, but nobody answered. That's funny, I thought. She's got to be in here. Mrs. Strickland said nobody'd seen her this morning. I knocked harder; I even called her. She couldn't have failed to hear me through those thin walls.

I saw the maid Cassie down by the broom closet. "Cassie!" I called. She came over. "Did you do this room today?"

She looked at me as if wondering why in the world I kept harping from time to time on whether she had done which rooms at what time. And she had a point there. I could see why she might wonder.

"Well, did you?" I was impatient.

"Yes, ma'am. Did it this morning, same as usual."

"Was Mrs. Nelson in then?"

"No, ma'am. Nobody was in."

"But Mrs. Nelson was sick. She must have been in."

"No, ma'am," Cassie repeated.

"Cassie, do you have your key? Open the door and let me be sure—did you do the bathroom too?"

"Yes, ma'am. Nobody was in the bathroom either." She got out her key and opened the door, coming in behind me. The room was neat—and vacant. My eyes swept around it.

The closet door was shut.

"Cassie," I whispered, "did you open the closet?"

"No, ma'am. No need to clean the closet. Wasn't no clothes lying around to hang up."

No. The clothes were still on Sophie Nelson. I opened the closet door. The stale smell of liquor aged in the stomach hit me in the face. On the floor a large crumpled bundle of flowered silk turned out to be Mrs. Nelson. "Another murder!" I gasped, and Cassie let out a yell and went screaming for help.

Before the crowd came, though, it had dawned on me that the alcoholic carbon-dioxide smell might possibly mean that Sophie was still breathing. I touched her, and she wasn't cold. She was limp and unconscious, but possibly alive. I didn't know whether to pull her out of the closet and try to revive her or to leave her alone and not touch anything. That seemed heartless, but I remembered from a first-aid class that sometimes when a person's injured it's best not to move her.

169

Fortunately I didn't have to decide. Mr. Bridgewater and a plainclothes cop arrived on the double, followed by at least half the population of the center. Mr. Bridgewater shut the door on them. "I think she's still alive," I said, fast. He pulled her out of the closet and hurriedly examined her. I gathered he had already phoned for the doctor and Lieutenant Ayres and the rest of the crew.

"Well, is she?" I asked anxiously. I had grown somewhat fond of old Sophie, too. I hoped she was all right.

"She's been hit in the back of the head *and* strangled," Mr. Bridgewater said. "He must have thought he had killed her, when he stuffed her in the closet. But her neck's so fat it must have kept the choking from killing her. She probably passed out and lay quiet in there more from the liquor than from the attack, and that fooled him into thinking she was dead. But she may have a nasty concussion from this blow, all the same. He probably hit her from behind, so she wouldn't recognize him."

"He needn't have hit her," I said angrily, getting a wet towel and kneeling to wipe Sophie's face, half expecting a reprimand. "She'd been drinking too much to remember him anyway, more than likely. And who would want to kill Mrs. Nelson? She was harmless—she didn't have a thing to do with the murders. The only things she cared about were the Bible and the bottle, and maybe her book." Poor old thing, lying in that closet all night and all morning, unconscious. If the building hadn't been so old and drafty and full of cracks, she couldn't even have breathed.

"She must have known something dangerous to the murderer, though," Mr. Bridgewater said soberly. "That's why I keep telling you, Libby, to stay out of all this. And don't be alone with any of 'em."

"I guess he got in through the window that opens on the gallery," I said. "Unless she left the door unlocked. She probably did—she was really very drunk last night. Not coherent at all the last time I saw her, and she was still drinking then."

"The screen's still fastened," Mr. Bridgewater said. "Probably he followed her in."

Lieutenant Ayres and his following arrived then. The ambulance beat Dr. Mabie here this time, and the young intern had a chance to use his stethoscope at last. They put Sophie on a stretcher and rushed her off to the hospital, and they rushed me right out of the room. So I couldn't watch them test for fingerprints and the rest of it. Lieutenant Ayres dispersed the crowd in the hall for the time being, with the familiar warning that he wanted to talk to everybody later. By common consent more than the Dean's, the workshops for this afternoon were called off. Most of the Writers buzzed around in the lobby, going over and over what they didn't know. Nobody admitted knowing anything. Nobody had seen Mrs. Nelson after Mrs. Strickland left her in her room alone about midnight.

More than half the conference crowd wanted to go home; they were frightened and appalled and didn't see that the conference had any business to continue until they were all murdered. But Lieutenant Ayres said nobody was to leave, and he made it clear that it was no use to try. Miss DeBrett said she intended to Sue Him if anybody Attacked her, but it didn't seem to worry him any. Dean Crossett announced that the concert would be held in the auditorium this evening, as scheduled.

After a while Lieutenant Ayres locked up Mrs. Nelson's

room, posted a guard, and came with his men to set up a question-and-answer bureau again in a vacant workshop room. But if he learned anything before going off to the Hawes inquest (to which I couldn't get an invitation) about five, I couldn't find out what. Mr. Bridgewater was gloomily mum, leaving for his supper without telling me anything except to be careful. I made him promise to let me know how Sophie was, as soon as the doctors determined how bad her injuries were. The intern had said he thought she'd be all right but that of course she might remain unconscious for a while.

Well, at least in the hospital she'd be safe from the murderer. But he must be getting desperate, I thought, if he was among us, realizing that he hadn't killed her after all—that whatever she had known that incriminated him she still knew.

12

Thursday Evening

There was time before supper for me to ask Nan Gorman
about the phone call, I decided. I had almost forgotten
that again. So much was always happening to sidetrack
me. I wouldn't want to be a detective for a life work.

"Nan," I said, "can you slip away for a minute and
come talk to me? Get Frank to hold down the switchboard
—he's not doing anything."

"All right," she said. Frank waved us away gracefully.
"Let's get a Coke, shall we?"

"Not now," I said. "I've got something important to ask
you, and it would be dangerous—for both of us—if anybody overheard it. Let's see—where can we go? Oh, one
of the workshop rooms would be all right. Nobody's going
to be up there until tomorrow."

We went up to 206; probably I picked it subconsciously because I'd been going to it every day for the mystery workshop. Nobody was there, of course; the table and chairs had the deserted look of a stage set after the actors have gone. I shut the door, and Nan and I sat down at one corner of the instructor's table.

"What's all this about you working on the murders?" Nan said curiously. "Frank was telling me you're playing detective."

"Nothing like that," I said. "I'm just trying to work it all up into a mystery book. For the workshop exercise, you know. So of course I have to find out all I can about what really happened. You may be able to give me one important bit of information that will clinch a case I've got worked up against one of the suspects." I thought how professional that sounded.

"I bet you want me to admit doing something you know I shouldn't," she said astutely. "If you weren't one of my best friends, I'd say no before you even ask me."

"But since you're curious about what it is, *and* a best friend, you won't say no," I assured her. "I won't tell the police. Though probably *you* ought to tell them."

"And admit I sometimes listen in? To keep from being bored? No, I don't think so, Libby."

"And I wouldn't put it in the book, of course," I went on, "until all this is over and the murderer is tried and found guilty. Anyway, I'll change all the names and nobody'll know the telephone operator is you."

"Tried—found guilty—and executed?" she breathed. It had a solemn, horrifying sound, there in the quiet everyday room, though probably there'd be no death penalty left anywhere by the time all his appeals were exhausted.

"Don't you think maybe he ought to be," I said, "for what he did to Kay Hawes? And now poor old Sophie Nelson?" I noticed objectively that I hadn't mentioned what he'd done to Carlton Gillespie.

"Poor Kay. Yes," Nan said soberly, reflectively. "I was talking to her just—day before yesterday. It doesn't seem possible she can be dead. But the funeral's to be tomorrow —if the police are through with her by then."

"She was a friend of yours, wasn't she?" I said sympathetically. "I remember you sometimes baby-sat for them. So you felt even worse about it than I did, probably—and I felt terrible. Because of *him*. Professor Hawes. He loved her so much. I'm a sucker for romance, you know. What were you and she talking about—the day she was killed?" I asked then. "Did it have anything to do with the murder?"

"Gossip," Nan said, shrugging. "The things I shouldn't tell—but being human, I do once in a while mention them to my closest friends, like you and Kay, because the bits are so interesting. She said I oughtn't to tell anybody this bit, though. She said it might get him in trouble, and he wasn't the one who ought to be—"

"Then it's probably the same thing I had in mind," I said excitedly. "Nan—you can tell *me*. Was it about the man Mr. Gillespie talked to on the phone Monday, early in the evening before he was killed? The man he was asking to pay back the money he'd loaned him, or else do the job he had for him?"

"How did you know that?" Nan was surprised. "You couldn't have been listening in. I was—I admit it, but not to anybody else. But you—"

"It wasn't on purpose," I explained. "I was trying to get

Frank on the line to get me some ice, and the wires were crossed somehow, and I overheard a small bit of the conversation. But I didn't recognize the other man's voice. You must know who he was."

"Yes," she admitted. "But—" Her voice had a dawning horror as she realized it. "I told Kay—and she was killed. It couldn't have been because of that—could it, Libby?"

"Yes," I had to say. "I'm afraid it could, Nan. She must have known something that was dangerous to the man who murdered Mr. Gillespie. This could have been it. So tell me quick—who was it?"

"And have you killed too? No, I won't—"

"Oh, come on," I said impatiently. "I'm not going to get killed. I'm alerted for it. Kay wasn't. And Sophie was too drunk to even know she was hit. But it can't happen to me. So tell me—who was he?"

"Mr. Gillespie—" Her voice was low and had a quality of denial even while she was damning him with the revelation, "called Mr. Hamlyn Brent's room."

Her face was still unbelieving and horror-stricken. But I had known all the time what she was going to say. It all fitted together now. I had needed to know why anyone would have wanted to kill Kay Hawes, and Nan had just told me why Hamlyn Brent might have. Because somehow he must have found out she knew this thing that would give him the motive for the killing of Carlton Gillespie. But she would have known how he felt; she had told Nan not to tell. . . . I felt sick, because I had looked at his long-fingered hands with that cigarette holder, and I didn't like to think of those long fingers closing tighter and tighter around a woman's throat. I didn't like to believe it. Because I had admired Hamlyn Brent.

176

"It fits, Nan. Sometime I'll tell you how perfectly. But —I wish it didn't. I wish you had said it was Van Saylor or Dory Pevlin or almost anybody but—him. I thought I wanted to get the final incriminating thing that would fit into the last hole in the puzzle—but now I wish—I wish I didn't have it so nicely wrapped up."

"What about Mrs. Nelson?" Nan asked. "Does he fit her case, too?"

Well, now, I thought, there's another loophole, maybe. Yesterday when I worked it all out for Mr. Brent to be the one, if only I could find a motive for him to have killed Kay Hawes, Mrs. Nelson hadn't yet been attacked. How could he have known she knew anything that could tell against him? Kay must have somehow let slip what *she* knew. Did Mrs. Nelson, too? I could see him conversing urbanely with Kay, but somehow I wouldn't have thought he'd have tolerated Sophie for a minute. So when—Did he happen to overhear something significant? He had said he could hear her when she talked in her room.

"I'll have to think about it," I answered Nan. "Right now I don't know. But I guess she may fit his case as well as anybody else." It was a painful surmise. "It's got to be that she was a threat to the one who killed Mr. Gillespie, too."

"This is interesting, but I've got to get back to the switchboard or Frank will murder me," she said, getting up—and then she realized what she had said. Frank would *murder*—She began to laugh almost hysterically. This strain was getting on all our nerves. "I've got to get back," she stammered again, hiccuping. "See you later, Libby. You be careful."

"You be careful yourself," I said soberly. "Kay Hawes

may not have let him know where she got her information —which would explain why you haven't been killed yet. Just keep very quiet about it, will you, Nan?"

"I sure will," she said fervently, and she was gone. I sat still a minute longer, trying to figure it out. I was looking down at the table, doodling idly and thinking madly, when I gradually realized that somebody else was in the room with me. I stopped breathing. Slowly I turned to see who it was.

Hamlyn Brent stood just inside the doorway.

He came in and closed the door behind him.

"Ah, Miss Clark," he said softly. "Working out some more clues, perhaps? Some more motives and opportunities?"

My heart was going like the Kentucky Derby. I almost screamed, but my throat was too dry and constricted for the sound to come out. I just stared at him and felt my dry tongue creep stealthily out to try to moisten my dry lips.

He moved around the table as if looking for something. "I thought perhaps I left my book here," he murmured, "but I don't see it." He moved back casually—perhaps accidentally?—to a spot between me and the only door to the room.

"I haven't seen it," I said at last, swallowing the nervous dread. I stood up, gathered my bag and other things together, and started toward the door.

"Don't go yet, Miss Clark." He pulled out a chair and sat in it, tilting it back so that it almost unintentionally blocked the way to the door. "Sit down, why don't you? Maybe there's time to talk over your book some more. Your ideas about murder interest me very much." That last sentence rang in my ears with a sinister echo—and kept on echoing.

I sat down. There didn't seem to be anything else to do. If he was insane—as anybody who would kill Kay Hawes and attack Sophie Nelson must be—I didn't want to antagonize him unnecessarily. At least, I told myself doubtfully, he didn't appear really violent at the moment.

"I'm glad the book sounds interesting to you," I answered lamely.

"I didn't exactly mean the book," he answered softly. "I just meant—the ingenious ideas you have."

I tried to keep my lips from quivering, my hands from shaking. I tried to look him straight in the eyes, with nonchalance that would assure him I wasn't afraid—indeed that I had nothing at all to be afraid of in Hamlyn Brent. But I don't think I'm a very good actress. I knew this floor of the building, with the assembly rooms and such, was deserted at this twilight hour. I knew he could overpower me without any trouble at all, with his hands on my throat preventing me from screaming until he had strangled me, too, if this was what he had in mind. Yes, he could kill me if he wanted to, and there wasn't a thing I could do to prevent it.

All of a sudden my self-control broke. In horror I heard my own voice, and I was helpless to stop it. "You did it, didn't you?" I babbled. "I won't tell the police—I haven't told them a thing—but you did it, I know. Didn't you? You owed Mr. Gillespie money—he was making you give him all your plots—write mysteries for him instead of for yourself. 'No man shall take the nether or the upper millstone to pledge, for he taketh a man's life to pledge.' "

The stream of significant facts I had gathered poured out of me damningly, giving him the best motive in the world for strangling me too. I could almost feel his hands on my throat already. But I couldn't stop the hysterical flow of words.

"He took your millstone—and you fought with him about it. Maybe you didn't mean to when you started—but you killed him. You were in the room next to mine—the door between wasn't locked until I came up to bed—you could have swapped the Bibles. You hadn't any alibi for midnight Monday. And I found out Kay Hawes knew about your motive for getting Mr. Gillespie out of the way. He was threatening you about money you owed him and the job you were doing for him—and Kay knew it. So—you had to kill her too. I knew the Bible verse had something to do with it!" I cried, breathing hard and painfully. "The others' motives are better—at least it would have been for love, not money, if Mel or Professor Hawes had done it. But you're the only one that every single thing fits —but I won't tell them—" I put my head down on the table as if it were the executioner's block, objectively feeling my tears on my wrists, dreading the next thing I must feel.

The silence, the waiting, were horrible.

After a while, when I hadn't yet felt any hands on my neck, I *had* to lift my head.

Mr. Brent was still leaning back in the tilted chair, still not-smoking the cigarette in the holder dangling from his fingers, still regarding me with that fiendish trace of amusement.

"And what have you figured out about Mrs. Nelson?"

he asked almost tolerantly. Oh, I thought. He has to find out everything I know, before he—

"Nothing," I gasped on the end of a sob. "That's the one reason I thought maybe you didn't—but there's probably something she knew that would clinch it. You said you often overheard her talking. You saw me with Mel in the lobby last night. That means you left the coffee shop soon after I did and were on your way upstairs. Sophie went to bed about midnight, Mrs. Strickland said. You could have followed her into her room all right, if she forgot to lock the door."

"Yes, I could," he acknowledged mockingly. "You've done a really remarkable job of putting two and two together. Too bad you got five," he said sardonically. "Yes, it's very nearly all true, too. And very ingenious, I may say, Miss Clark. I must congratulate you. I think you have a future in the mystery fiction field, quite definitely.

"But your plot unfortunately falls down in one respect as a solution to the actual crimes. It *is* fiction. I'm not the only one every single thing fits. The facts have to fit one other person too—the murderer. Because, Miss Clark, I didn't kill them."

There it was again, just as when I'd eliminated Mel and Professor Hawes and Van Saylor from my list of suspects. I *believed* him. Instinctively, deep in my subconscious, I guess I had thought all the time that he wasn't a murderer. Or I wouldn't have sat there like a—like a hysterical woman—and given him all that reason to kill me.

"You didn't?" I said dumbly.

Then I began to laugh, from sheer relief and hysteria and release from tension. I shut my eyes and put my head down on the table again and giggled like a moron, crying at the same time.

Suddenly I felt a hand touch my cheek. He was leaning over me; I could hear him breathing. I froze; I stopped laughing and crying; I was warily still, like an animal the moment it senses the gun aimed.

His long-fingered hands lifted my head, cupped my cheeks between his palms. I almost felt his fingers slide down to my throat. But no. He was looking deeply, compellingly, into my eyes, and his were the most astonishing green, a green that was almost black. I had never noticed that deep green of his eyes before.

"Libby," he said, and this time there was a powerful throbbing intensity in his voice, and no trace of mockery at all. "Listen to me. *I did not kill them.*"

At last I gulped and whispered, "All right. I'm—glad."

I found a tissue and wiped my face and blew my nose.

"Now listen," he said sternly, sitting in the chair beside me. "You haven't a grain of sense, or you wouldn't have told me all that ingenious rot you figured out about why I killed two people and attacked a third. Don't you see, if I really had, it would have meant you'd be the fourth victim?"

"I see," I said meekly. "I knew all that, of course, but I—I just couldn't help it. It seemed I just had to get it all out in the open. I guess I really did flip for a minute." For lack of something intelligent to say, I got out my compact and lipstick and repaired my face.

"Since I didn't kill them," he went on thoughtfully, "we'll have to revise your reasoning a little. There must be someone else here who has just as powerful motives as those you attributed to me"—he was back into the irony again now—"or perhaps even more powerful. One thing —you said I must have been the one who swapped the Bibles, preparing that verse for Gillespie earlier in the evening, because I had the room next to yours and the door between was unlocked all evening. Well, that's one place your assumption was wrong, Miss Clark." I thought in the back of my head, maybe a bit wistfully, he called me Libby a while ago. Now it was back to Miss Clark and the sardonic note again.

"Wrong?" I said. "I know the door was unlocked—I thought about it after I went to bed, and found it unlocked when I tried it. While you were in the bathroom—at least, the water was running. That was when I locked it."

"I had the room then, yes," he said. "But I had just moved into that room a little after ten o'clock Monday night. I had four-oh-eight, and the place was full, and that boy Frank what's-his-name asked me if I'd like a corner room instead of the one I had—if I'd mind changing with somebody who had some fool temperamental reason for not wanting this one *because* it's a corner room. I like a corner room better, naturally—there are two windows and cross ventilation. I had asked him about getting one, when I registered, but none was vacant. So of course I was willing to change."

"Who—" I said faintly, "who was it wanted to change?"

"I don't know. I don't think the clerk said—or if he did I wasn't paying any attention. The man had already moved his things when I took mine in. But we can find out by asking that clerk at the desk."

183

"Yes!" I said. "I remember now—I was subconsciously bothered by something about your having this room. Now I remember. You didn't fit the person I saw going in the door as I was coming in when I first got here. It was only a glimpse of his back, and I can't even bring up the image now." I stopped; something else was knocking at me to be remembered. What else? What else? I had heard the water running before I opened the door between . . .

"Do you believe I'm telling you the truth about not killing anybody?" he asked gravely.

I had heard the water running—but I *hadn't* heard him talking on the phone to Mr. Gillespie earlier. He had admitted being the man who was talking to Mr. Gillespie. Nan had said Mr. Gillespie had called Mr. Brent's room. If he had been in the next room I must have heard the conversation through the wall, at least imperfectly, as well as over the crossed wires. I hadn't heard any voice at all, besides those on the phone.

Therefore, he wasn't in the next room.

He was telling the truth. Somebody else had had that room at the time the Bibles could have been changed.

"Yes. I believe you," I said.

"So now," he said very seriously, "we've got to find out who else had a nether millstone that Carlton Gillespie had been putting his thieving hands on."

It was a very comforting little word, that small two-letter "we."

13

Still Thursday Evening

It was frustrating to find no clerk at all at the desk when we went down. I had figured it was Frank's evening off, but I thought there'd be somebody we could ask about who changed rooms with Mr. Brent.

"He's bound to be back soon," Mr. Brent said. "If he's not, when we get through supper we'll find the registration cards ourselves and look. But now hadn't we better get something to eat before the dining room closes?"

"All right," I agreed. There could be no harm in letting it go until I saw Frank again, really. I could call his frat house after supper.

It was late; almost everybody else had finished and the dining room was nearly empty. Mel and Carla were at an inconspicuous table; obviously they had come down late to escape the crowd. Mrs. Gillespie must still be having meals in her room, I thought.

"Shall we sit with them?" I said, and Mr. Brent agreed. I noted with a certain amount of self-congratulation that he was coming out of his smug, aloof, observer-bystander shell gradually—if our near-collaboration could go on a little longer, he might be almost human.

Mel stood up as we approached and said, "Won't you sit with us?" before we could even suggest it. Mr. Brent hadn't met Carla before, and I could see he thought her an attractive girl, even though she was pale and obviously still grieving. I had to be careful about what I said, I realized, because Mel didn't know all the things I knew about Mr. Brent and Mr. Gillespie, and there was no need for him to know. Or Carla. There was no need for anybody to know now about Mr. Brent's humiliating ghost-writing, and I was glad.

We ordered, and while waiting I told them I'd like to go and phone to find out how Mrs. Nelson was getting along.

Dory Pevlin was idling near the phone booth, and I said hello.

"Look," he said abruptly, "I want you to forget all that damn nonsense I was spouting about killing by psychokinesis. Will you?"

"Don't tell me Lieutenant Ayres believes it?" I asked with interest. "I'd never have thought you could persuade *him.* Is he about to arrest you?"

"No. I don't think so. It's not that. It's just—oh, hell, I can't feel like that about these last two things. I mean, it was all very well to be glad—and pose like that—when it was that heel Gillespie. But Mrs. Hawes and that poor old girl in the hospital—I wouldn't even think about them at all, much less think their death. So you see, the other was just wishful thinking." He was so serious about it that I had to restrain an urge to laugh.

"Why don't you put your mental powers to work on getting Mrs. Nelson well, then?" I said. "Then maybe she could tell whatever it is she knows that might identify the real murderer. I was just going to phone the hospital about how she is."

He looked at me with pitying disdain and wandered away. He was certainly a strange boy, I mused as I looked up the hospital number.

They told me with professional objectivity that Mrs. Nelson's condition was serious but she was not on the critical list. The information clerk let me speak to the floor nurse, who said Mrs. Nelson was still unconscious and that a detective was waiting to speak to her as soon as she could talk. Lieutenant Ayres had the inside track there, all right.

I tried to get Frank at his frat house, but no luck. I left a message. The other clerk still wasn't back at the desk. Oh, well, it was just one detail. It wouldn't prove anything even when we found out who it was who changed rooms that night. But it might point the way.

I saw Mr. Bridgewater just outside in the courtyard, moodily feeding the pigeons crumbs and peanuts. I went to speak to him.

"What's new? I can't get the hospital to tell me confidentially anything about poor old Sophie except the regular routine bulletin."

"They think she'll be all right," he said. "Doc Mabie says she's plenty tough. Well-preserved. Like an Exhibit A kept in alcohol."

"Well, what else goes on down at headquarters?"

"You know I can't say, Libby." Then his wish to show his inside knowledge got a slight edge on his discretion. "But I'll tell you this much, Dopey's about to make an arrest."

"Who? Poor Mr. Hawes?"

"I can't say." And this time he really wouldn't. But I was afraid it was Mr. Hawes. Unless Mr. Brent and I could prove it was somebody else.

As I went back to the dining room I met Mrs. Strickland. "I've had the most exciting time," she said. "I had to go to the inquest—Mrs. Hawes, you know—because I found her, and then I went to the hospital to see Sophie, only they wouldn't let me see her because she's still unconscious—"

"Come on and sit with us and tell us about it while we eat," I said. "My supper's getting cold. Have you eaten yet?"

"No, I just got back from the hospital. The taxi man wanted to talk about the murder too. All right, I believe I will have something. I wasn't going to that concert anyway." Dean Crossett was doggedly promoting the concert, just as if nothing unusual had happened at this conference.

The group of late eaters had grown while I was away from the table. They were the only ones left in the dining room, and two tables had been pushed together to make room for Van Saylor and Elaine Westover, of all people, to join the party. I wondered who had invited them—and why they'd accepted. Maybe they just came in and invited themselves. I couldn't imagine Mel or Carla or Mr. Brent asking them. But I'd have thought that if Van Saylor had managed to persuade Miss Westover to have a late supper with him, he'd rather it would have been just the two of them. Maybe it was that she'd rather be with almost anybody else than alone with Mr. Saylor. But he wasn't that bad, I thought. At least when he was wearing something else instead of that green plaid jacket. He looked quite toned down, in gray striped seersucker. But she probably inflamed him more than I did.

All this was running on palpitating little feet through my mind as Mrs. Strickland and I approached the table.

"Mr. Bridgewater says the police are about to make an arrest," I announced as Mel and Mr. Brent stood up, and Van Saylor belatedly did too after considering it—it seemed—for a long moment. They placed chairs for us, with an interested questioning of "Who?" from everybody.

"He won't say. But it might be Mr. Hawes, mightn't it?"

"Weren't they watching him when Mrs. Nelson was attacked?" Mr. Brent said. "They should have been, if they suspected him."

"You're right about that," I admitted doubtfully but with some hope. "Maybe that'll clear him."

Mrs. Strickland gave her order to the waitress as soon as she had settled down next to me. It looked like any cozy little group of writers—the same kind that so often gathers at such conferences as this. You know—a few people will sit together and some more acquaintances will come along and be invited to join them, and the circle gradually widens, and more tables are pushed together, and the conversation becomes general, and after a while everybody's having a wonderful time, and the waitresses who have been hovering around for quite a while just give up on the idea that they'll ever be able to get rid of the literary freaks so they can clear up and relax a few minutes before they have to prepare the place for the next meal.

But this little group wasn't such a cozy one. Carla was withdrawn and gloomy; Mel smiled only at me, and that briefly; Mr. Brent had become the people-watcher again; Miss Westover had adopted a superficially youthful attitude that was sickening. Van Saylor was in there trying, but with a very heavy hand, and I was mostly eating my roast beef and green salad. Mrs. Strickland was the only one who really wanted to talk, and I thought what a help she was at breaking up the uncomfortable silences.

"She was still unconscious," she answered Miss Westover's idle inquiry about Sophie Nelson. "Poor Sophie. Who could have wanted to hurt *her?*"

"Even if she knew anything incriminating," Van Saylor said thoughtfully, "she probably didn't know she knew it. She was usually so befuddled that it wouldn't have meant much—to her *or* the police. She'd have forgotten it by the time she was sober again. I doubt if the evidence of a drunk is admissible anyway."

"What you say is very likely true," Hamlyn Brent observed, "but you can't be sure she would have forgotten it. The murderer couldn't be sure she would, either. So he silenced her—or thought he had."

"I think you all are being cruel about Sophie," Mrs.

Strickland championed stoutly. "She wasn't always—what you said. Sometimes she showed very good sense. I met her only this week, but we've already gotten to be good friends. She was the one who figured out the Bible verse for the police, remember?" Mrs. Strickland was wearing the joe-pye-weed thing again this evening, and her walnut-tinted hair made a weird bright-brown halo for her flushed face. But I liked her for sticking up for Sophie.

"You went to the inquest on poor Kay late this afternoon," I reminded. "What happened?"

"Well, not very much. They had it in that furniture store, of all places. Well, in the funeral parlor part of the furniture store. They had what they called a jury, of very odd-looking people, and they went and *looked* at her." Her voice sank disapprovingly. " 'Viewing the body,' they called it. As if it were a scenic vista or something. And only one woman in the bunch. They had had an autopsy and decided she was strangled. As if anybody couldn't see that! Even I could tell she was strangled when I first saw her. And they asked poor Professor Hawes a lot of questions. How all this must be upsetting his writing! How could he ever concentrate on the Third Crusade again with all this happening right in his own family! I know it's all I can do to get my mind back on Tom Jefferson even when he's all I'm thinking about."

"Back to the inquest, Mrs. Strickland," I said gently.

"Well, they asked me a lot of foolish questions too." She flushed and skipped the one about why she was going to that rest room. "And Mr. Phillips too—he seems to have been the last person to see her alive—except the murderer, of course. You were the next-to-last, weren't you, Libby?"

"I guess so. But they didn't call me for this inquest.
. . . But what about Mrs. Nelson? She said she saw Kay
talking to somebody else—and then actually saw her go
into the auditorium."

"That's why they wanted to wait until Sophie gets able
to tell them a few things," Mrs. Strickland said. "They
decided to adjourn it or postpone it or whatever the legal
term is, until she can be a witness. Even if she *was* drinking
a little. So they let us all go until then."

"Do they think this murder of Mrs. Hawes and the
attack on Mrs. Nelson were all connected with Mr. Gillespie's murder?" Elaine Westover asked in her slow, smooth
voice. It was a voice like raw silk, smooth but with now
and then a small irregularity, like a heavier thread or slub
in the silk, to catch the attention.

"Nobody knows what they think," grunted Van Saylor.
I was surprised that Miss Westover showed so little emotion in speaking of Mr. Gillespie's murder. After all, she
had been by repute—if you could call it that—one of his
closest women friends at the time of his death. But she
seemed to have no feeling at all about it now. Carla Gillespie, though, struggled with her private woe, flinching at
the mention of her father.

"If they could only find out who it was he was planning
to meet in the garden Monday night, they'd just about
have the murderer, wouldn't they?" Miss Westover pursued pensively. "And then we could all go home. If only
he'd told me who it was—"

"You mean he told you he was meeting someone late
that night?" Mr. Brent leaned forward, a glint in his eye.
He had long ago finished eating. "Miss Westover, that

could be important. Mrs. Gillespie thought—" He stopped, with belated delicacy.

"But he didn't tell me who," the poetess said earnestly, looking soulfully into Mr. Brent's green eyes, and I could tell she would rather have him panting after her than Van Saylor. As who wouldn't? "I was with him, yes, for a few minutes just before he went out into the garden that night. It couldn't be important—I told the police. He said he had to meet a writer who wanted to talk to him about adapting his latest *Redbook* story for television."

"It was an odd time and place for that," I said. Mentally I reviewed Larry Mims and Cobb Wilmer, the two who were holding drama workshops, and I couldn't fit them in at all.

"Gil would have talked to *any*body *any* time *any* place about his own work," Miss Westover said with lazy cynicism. "It didn't seem at all odd for him to be keeping the appointment then, if that's what you mean."

"Of course," I said, "it was probably just a dodge to get him out there alone. Probably had nothing to do with actually adapting a story for TV. Or he might have been lying to you for some good reason." It might have been another woman he was meeting for nothing more than a late date, but I didn't actually say that.

"I think you're right," Hamlyn Brent said—to both of us, I guess. "But, Miss Westover, are you sure he didn't give you any idea of who the person was?"

"No, he didn't. He liked to keep people in suspense, holding off, teasing them in order to make them beg to be confided in. I didn't beg enough."

"Yes, that fits," he meditated. "It fed his ego even more

193

that way. . . . You said you did tell the police about this, Miss Westover?"

"Of course." Elaine Westover shrugged. "But without the name of the person, what could they do with it?"

Such idle conversation, I thought. But then, nobody was much interested in going to that concert Dean Crossett had been plugging.

Mr. Brent said ruminatively, "Let's do a bit of brainstorming, shall we? Let's go back to that night—Monday night. Everybody try to remember now if there's anything at all that happened that seemed odd or that could possibly be connected with why Mr. Gillespie went out into the garden at midnight—anything that hasn't already been kicked around thoroughly."

Mrs. Strickland had finished eating and was fanning herself excitedly, the fan moving faster and faster as her mind followed the mystery like a bloodhound nosing a trail. "That night"—She frowned with the effort to remember, and because the memory did not fit, after all —"when Mr. Phillips left Sophie and me, he said he had to go because he had a conference with a writer. It could have been—but that was *after* twelve-five. After the murder had already been done. Maybe twenty or thirty minutes after. And people are always having individual conferences with the staff at the oddest hours—Miss DeBrett said she was having one with Ms. Ruskin at that time—"

Reminded by the name, Carla said listlessly to her brother, "I suppose I ought to hunt up Mr. Phillips and speak to him. He's Dale's father, you know, and she wanted to come with me, but when she phoned him he said he'd rather she stayed in school. Imagine—he said the trip would cost too much—"

"Dale who?" Mrs. Strickland was slightly hard of hearing, as well as nearsighted, but she would no more have worn a hearing aid than she would have appeared in public in glasses. But still she didn't want to miss anything. "Dale Barlow. She's a friend of mine at college. Mr. Phillips's daughter. He's always used his writing name, Dale says, ever since he got fired from a newspaper he used to work for because he protested over something very unfair that somebody there did to him."

"I know what you mean," Mrs. Strickland said sympathetically. "Somebody cut his throat behind his back." I gave Hamlyn Brent my smile over that one.

"The other person—whoever it was—had more influence with the paper's publisher than he did, so Mr. Phillips got fired for objecting to whatever it was they did," Carla said. She didn't even connect what she was saying with what I had asked her mother about earlier. "He was bitter about it and didn't even try to get another job. He nearly drank himself to death, Dale says, and her mother died, and then later he got hold of himself and started writing under the name of Phillips. And another pen name, too—I forget what that was. He didn't want to see anybody ever again that he'd ever known before. But he lets Dale use their real name, since she wants to. And he's ashamed of the kind of things he writes—he doesn't want her embarrassed by being connected with it. But she doesn't mind telling about it. It doesn't matter as much to her as it does to her father."

"Barlow!" Van Saylor said into the hush that followed. "Barlow. That's the name I couldn't remember. Paul Barlow. The reporter who did the work on the series Gillespie got the credit for—the Forrester Prize series—"

195

Carla started to speak indignantly, but Mel put a tense hand on hers and held it, and she kept quiet.

"But if *he's* Phillips—well, a beard can certainly change a man's appearance, no doubt about it. And he wasn't bald then, either. But I saw him only once or twice—I've forgotten how he looked then, actually—" Mr. Saylor was merely reminiscing. He actually didn't see the significance of what he and Carla had just said. The nether millstone. An embittered man—a very twisted, embittered man whose wife's death had resulted—he was convinced—from this injustice. The nether millstone.

I nearly choked on the swallow of coffee I had just taken before *I* connected.

"Paul!" I cried. "It wasn't the Bible Paul at all. The one Mrs. Nelson was babbling about wasn't Saul of Tarsus who afterward became Paul. (That's why she was attacked; he was at the table next to us and heard her.) The man she was identifying as talking to Kay Hawes just before she went into the auditorium—the one who could have followed her in and—yes, Mrs. Nelson had to have heard her call him Paul. See—Kay had recognized him from the old days when they worked on the paper together —with Mr. Gillespie. She could have exclaimed something that let him know she was putting two and two together about the Bible verse—"

Frank Benton came toward us at that psychological moment, threading his way around the maze of empty tables. "Joe said you called me, Libby?" he inquired. Then he turned to Carla. "Your mother asked me if I saw you to please tell you she's looking for you."

She couldn't have wanted to go at this point. I know

Mel wouldn't have. But he said, "See about Mother, please, Carla?" and she went.

Dazed with my own excitement, I forgot what it was I had been going to ask Frank about. "But—but—" Mrs. Strickland was stammering.

But Mr. Brent remembered. He had connected, too. "Frank," he said quietly, "you remember when you asked me Monday night to change rooms with some temperamental writer? Who was it that wanted to change? I've forgotten, if you told me at the time."

"Why, it was Mr. Phillips. I remembered you had asked for a corner room when you came in, Mr. Brent, and there weren't any corner ones vacant right then. So when Mr. Phillips wanted to change that night—said cross ventilation gave him a cold, of all the fool excuses—I thought about you, naturally. And—well, you said the room was all right when I asked you next day—"

"It was all right," Mr. Brent said softly. "Thanks, Frank."

"Mr. Phillips could have changed the Bibles." I was working frantically at the jigsaw puzzle now, though nobody but Mr. Brent had enough of the pieces to follow me. "Yes, when Cassie said the gentleman in three-twenty-seven was in at about nine, she meant Mr. Phillips, not you, Mr. Brent. That was before I saw him talking to Frank when I went down. Then he would have been asking to have his room changed, thinking that nobody would remember or notice that it made any difference."

"You mean," Mel said slowly, "that you think Jim Phillips could have killed Gil?"

"But he couldn't have," Mrs. Strickland said, fanning

197

away madly. "Don't you remember, Libby, we had an alibi, Sophie and Mr. Phillips and I? Sophie and I were actually talking with him in the coffee shop at the time of the murder."

I remembered the thing the mystery writers' handbook had stressed: if you've eliminated all the possible answers, then it has to be what remains. The impossible one.

But how?

"Your watch must have been wrong, Mrs. Strickland. It must have been fast."

"I told you before, Libby," she answered indignantly, "my watch keeps perfect time. I have to keep it right because I'm too nearsighted to see a clock. I have it checked regularly at that jeweler's on Peachtree Street who checks the railroad men's watches, what few of them are left. And the radio and television people's too."

I reached over and stopped her fanning hand.

I turned her wrist toward me and looked at her watch, and then at mine. My heart nearly stopped beating with the surge of excitement that pumped my blood hard against it.

"Mrs. Strickland," I said, choking on my words, "your watch is an hour fast."

"It can't be." She was positive; she just refused to believe it.

Suddenly the whole thing dawned on me. Peachtree Street—of course—

"Annabel Strickland," I said, "didn't anybody ever tell you that there's a time change between Atlanta and Alabama? Atlanta has Eastern Daylight-Saving Time and Alabama has Central Daylight-Saving Time. *There's an hour's difference.* You didn't turn your watch back an hour when you got here, did you?" Of course it was assumed that everybody knew.

"No—" Her vague eyes were wide and bewildered. "I didn't know I was supposed to. So that's why I always got to everything early," she said plaintively.

"Then when you thought it was twelve o'clock—and it *was* in Atlanta—when you and Mrs. Nelson were talking with Mr. Phillips in the coffee shop for another fifteen minutes or so—it was really only eleven o'clock here in Alabama. He could have been with you until after eleven-thirty and still have gone down to the garden by twelve-five."

Mr. Brent was on his feet, speaking to Frank Benton: "He's still in four-oh-eight—the room I moved from?"

"Yes, sir. Unless he went to the concert or somewhere."

"I doubt if *any*body went to the concert except Dean Crossett," Mr. Brent said sardonically, moving fast toward the door.

We took the elevator up; Frank cussed it adequately. He left it standing there open, when the whole crowd of us rushed out of it to see if Mr. Phillips was in his room. Because the elevator door as usual wouldn't close.

I suppose subconsciously we must have believed there's safety in numbers. Not one of us gave a thought to calling Lieutenant Ayres.

14

And Later
Thursday Evening

Outside 408 we paused, and I was reminded of a pack of neophyte hunting dogs not quite certain what is expected of them.

"The moment of truth," I whispered—trite, I admit—and Mr. Brent shot me a quizzical glance, and I was sorry I'd said it. Then he knocked with his knuckles on the door. It was a sharp, loud sound in the fusty stillness, and I realized we were all holding our breath.

Somebody stirred inside, and then a voice said wearily and almost with resigned expectation, "Come in." With sudden intuition I realized that he had been knowing this time of discovery would come sometime, and dreading it. Why didn't he try to leave, then? Why didn't he make some excuse and slip away? Because Lieutenant Ayres had men watching the center to be sure nobody did make a break for it? No—all at once it came to me with pitying certainty that he had thought he had to take that chance of not being discovered, because he needed the money he would get for being a speaker at the conference. For Dale. He had to try to stick it out until they paid him.

Mr. Brent opened the door, and we all crowded into the room. It was a shame, I thought obscurely—but I didn't suggest that we leave. No, I stood there and watched curiously, just like the rest.

Mr. Phillips glanced up defensively from where he sat on the edge of the bed. "What do you want?" He was in trousers and shirt with the sleeves rolled up; his arms looked thin and bony. But his hands—I couldn't take my eyes off his hands. They were very large. They looked plenty strong. I was glad there didn't seem to be any weapons around. But Mr. Phillips couldn't have been the gunman type of killer.

"Just to talk to you," Mr. Brent said. "There are some things you may be able to explain."

"What things? Why should I—" Mr. Phillips had gotten up now and was restlessly moving about the room. His eyes darted with a kind of dark panic from one to the other of us; his lips were pallid above the graying hairs of his beard.

"Did you?" I couldn't wait for Mr. Brent to go on. "Did you meet Mr. Gillespie in the garden that night and—"

Suddenly the man leaped past me, past Mrs. Strickland, who stood nearest the open door, and ran down the corridor. We were after him in an astonished moment, Mel and Mr. Brent in the lead, Van Saylor staying protectingly near Miss Westover. I was close behind Mr. Brent.

Mr. Phillips saw the open elevator standing there invitingly, hesitated for an instant, forgot the crucial thing about that elevator, and was lost. It was what anybody being chased would have done. He slipped inside it and clanged the metal grill behind him (it worked this time), caging himself as effectively as any animal in a zoo. I knew it—the outer door (that had to be closed before the elevator would start) refused to budge, just as it always did when I tried to operate it.

He stood there helplessly tugging at it. We couldn't possibly reach him, even if we had wanted to—and I doubt that any of us did. But he couldn't get away.

"Mr. Phillips—Mr. Paul Barlow—" Mr. Brent said softly and—it almost seemed—with compassion, "hadn't you better give up? I don't think you stand a chance of escape."

"I suppose so." But he didn't open the grill door. It might have worked if he had kept at it, but he didn't even try. He just stood there, his gaunt face working. "Yes, I should pay—for killing Kay Warden. Not for killing Carlton Gillespie. He took my work—lost my job for me—he made me the cause of my wife's death. He deserved to die, but I didn't actually mean to kill him at that time and place. All I meant to do was scare him into confessing that he had taken my work when he accepted the Forrester Prize years ago. I came here with that in mind."

"You knew he'd be here." Mr. Brent helped him along.

"That's why I accepted when they asked me to come." He nodded at Mr. Brent eagerly, as if glad to find that somebody understood. "This was the first time a good opportunity had come to pay him back. I was going to force him to admit, in his speech at the banquet, that he had wrongfully taken the prize for work I had done. If he wouldn't, I would stand up and denounce him right there.

"I was Phillips—the name didn't mean anything to him. I had changed; he didn't recognize me. And I kept out of his way all day Monday. I tried to stay in the background generally, though there was nobody else here who had known me in the old days except Kay Warden." He looked down at his hands, and shuddered, and put them behind him. Then he looked back at Mr. Brent.

"As Phillips I called him and asked him to meet me in the garden that night to talk about permission to adapt one of his early stories for television. He'd believe anything for publicity.

"That apt verse from Deuteronomy I noticed when Miss Clark left me at the mercy of Mrs. Nelson, there at the picnic supper, when she was ranting on about the Laws. I clipped it out of the Bible in my room and put it between two pieces of cellophane tape. I was going to show it to Gil, quote it to him, force him to acknowledge —yes, threaten to kill him if he didn't acknowledge in his banquet speech—" His tongue moved over his lips; I knew his mouth must be dry. "I put the cut Bible in the room next to mine, and then it occurred to me to change rooms so that—"

"Then you did mean to kill him," Mr. Brent said, "or you wouldn't have worn gloves. You'd have left fingerprints on that Bible."

"I meant to kill him, yes!" he said fiercely. "With my bare hands if he wouldn't do what I asked. Not with any weapon. I thought there was no use taking chances on fingerprints in case I had to kill him. It could have been a fair fight if he'd been that kind of man. But I'd a million times rather he'd been willing to make restitution—to stand up at that banquet and tell everybody that the Forrester Prize should have been mine." He smiled; it was a horrible thing to watch, pitiful because it was *proud*. "They'll know now, though," he realized. "Even if—I die for it—they'll know why—"

Mel couldn't stand it any longer. He went and shook the elevator door with such anger that it opened, meekly. All he felt about his stepfather he put into that shaking.

"Come out of there," he said gruffly. "A man shouldn't look like he's in a cage." I loved Mel for doing that.

But Mr. Phillips went on talking; now he was talking to Mel as the one who understood. "But at the moment I killed him I didn't know I was doing it. He made me mad. I was so furious with him and his calm way of assuming that nobody would believe me if I exposed him, that I went out of my head with rage. I found myself with my hands around his neck, choking him to death and beating his head on the stone at the same time. I had chosen that place to meet him, you see, because of the millstone. When I came to and realized he was dead, I put the Bible verse on his chest for an epitaph and slipped away. I got to my room without being seen. I tried—of course—to figure out some way to avoid being caught. Because of Dale." I thought there were tears in his eyes, but I wasn't sure.

Mel said, "Aren't you coming out?" and I realized that Mr. Phillips hadn't even left the elevator, though the door stood open. That was how hopeless he was.

He came out then and stood irresolutely in the narrow

space of hall in front of his accusers. But he had to go on talking, and not one of us thought to advise him that he had a right to an attorney before he confessed. He probably wouldn't have cared; he had a compulsion now to talk, to justify, or explain if he couldn't justify, the things he had done.

"It wouldn't matter much about me," he went on sadly. "My work for that Forrester Prize would have been recognized at last, and I'm going to die in a few months anyhow. I've got cancer."

He sounded almost glad, poor man.

The stark statement left us all speechless for a moment. Then Mrs. Strickland said mechanically, "I'm sorry—" and Mel muttered, "Tough luck—"

But Hamlyn Brent said, "Congratulations," and Mr. Phillips gave him another grateful-for-understanding look.

"It was because of Dale that I hoped, as soon as I thought about it, to avoid being named a murderer." He went on, "It was lucky for me that Mrs. Strickland believed I'd been talking with her at the time Gil's watch stopped. I never thought of an alibi until she said that. But the police automatically struck me off their list of suspects. I felt reprieved, as though Fate might be on my side. I thought maybe I could even stay the week out and get the fee the conference pays staff members. I needed it." I nodded to myself; I had figured that.

He was denouncing himself now, quietly, painfully. "I was a fool to panic when Kay Warden recognized me. It's no use to say now that I wish that hadn't happened. If I'd only stopped to think when I followed her into the auditorium—to talk to her—she might not have told what she knew. He'd stolen her work, too. Later I heard somebody talking about that novel of his, and the title came from a poem she'd written a long time ago. I might be the only person who'd remember it now—

"But all I could think of then was that I was afraid of being caught and hurting Dale. I panicked. I've always panicked. Maybe I'm psycho—they wouldn't have me in the Army. Anyway, I blacked out again and came to with my hands around her throat and her dead." He shuddered. "I can't bear it—that I did that." He put his face in his hands. "But it was the same way when I heard Mrs. Nelson mention the name Kay had called me—Paul. They'd know about Gillespie. I panicked."

He paused a moment, and Mr. Brent, moved by some obscure compassion, lit his ready, unlit cigarette and handed it to him. He took it, said, "Thank you," automatically, and let it burn out in his hand.

"What do we do now?" I asked Mr. Brent helplessly. The others were murmuring among themselves; Frank Benton said something about telephoning.

"I guess we'll have to," Mr. Brent agreed. "If he'd only stopped at Gillespie, it might have been called second-degree murder or self-defense or manslaughter if they were fighting— There's also such a defense as 'irresistible impulse'; it was used in *Anatomy of a Murder,* remember? But he did kill Kay Hawes, even though he wishes he hadn't."

"It was unpremeditated, though," I offered, remembering the phrase from the handbook. "Won't that help?" I noted with objective wonder that I was talking about help

—for a murderer. But he seemed to have thrown himself on our mercy. Not that it would do him any good, even if we all should feel merciful. "Or maybe he was temporarily insane. He said he sort of blacked out."

"Maybe," Mr. Brent said cynically. "But it'd take a good lawyer for his defense."

Before anybody else could offer a suggestion or comment, we heard heavy footsteps on the stairs that opened from a fire door at the corner of the corridor close by. It sounded like an army coming up. The fire door opened, and Mr. Bridgewater, Lieutenant Ayres, and several cops and detectives swarmed around us.

"What the hell—" Lieutenant Ayres said, catching sight of Mr. Phillips. "You people can explain later," he said grimly to the lot of us. Then he said sonorously to Mr. Phillips, "Paul Barlow, alias James Phillips, alias Phillip James, I have a warrant for your arrest in the murder of Carlton Gillespie and Kay Hawes."

They took Mr. Phillips away, and he was abjectly begging Dopey, "James Phillips, please. Not Barlow. Please."

Mr. Bridgewater stayed behind when the rest of the headquarters squad left.

"How in the world," I asked him, "did Lieutenant Ayres know Mr. Phillips was the one? How did he solve the whole thing just like that? He didn't know all this stuff we found out about him—and the rest—" I looked at Mr. Brent, who shrugged a sardonic shoulder.

"Routine stuff," Mr. Bridgewater said. "Real murders hardly ever make good stories, Libby. This one was solved just the way most of them are solved, by routine police work. Dopey found people at the newspaper who remembered Barlow and supplied the motive for Gillespie's murder, after Dopey knew he was the one who killed Kay Hawes. He thinks he can break that alibi for Barlow without too much trouble."

"We already did that," I said. "We'll be glad to clue Lieutenant Ayres in on it. But how did he know Mr. Phillips killed Kay Hawes?"

"Routine investigation, like I said," Mr. Bridgewater answered. "His fingerprints clinched it. The first killing, he didn't leave any prints. But when he killed Kay Hawes he wasn't expecting to and he didn't wear gloves. His fingerprints were on the inside doorknob of the rest room where her body was found."

"But anybody's fingerprints could be on a rest-room door," Van Saylor pondered stupidly, looking at his own hands as if wondering whether one should wear gloves under all circumstances, however unlikely.

"This was the ladies' room," Mr. Bridgewater said.

As we walked down the stairs—because no amount of cussing could make the elevator move an inch, Frank found out—I said thoughtfully, "I don't think I really want to be a mystery writer after all. I feel too sorry for the villain. Maybe everything is predestined—and he was pushed into it by circumstances—"

"All right," Mel said, putting his arm around me. "You don't have to write murder mysteries."

But Hamlyn Brent said, "You'll do all right, Libby." (So I was Libby again.) He put another cigarette into his holder and didn't light it, as we paused for breath on the second-floor landing. "You'll just have to make your murderer a less sympathetic character, that's all."

"I tried hard enough," I said ruefully. "But he turned out to be sort of sympathetic, too. Actually," I said with a smile, "I was going to have him be a guy named John Smith."

Mel didn't know what I was talking about. But Hamlyn did.